THE
COLLECTION

A NOVELLA

BY

KATHERINE SILVA

Trigger warnings: Blood, warfare, death, needles, mental illness, dental trauma, abuse, hospitalization, PTSD, smoking

This book is a work of fiction. Anything that bears resemblance to real people, places, or events is entirely coincidental and unintentional.

Kindle 1st Edition: April 2018
Kindle 2nd Edition: March 2022

Paperback 1st Edition: April 2018
Paperback 2nd Edition: March 2022

Cover photo courtesy of pexels.com

Cover Design by Katherine Silva
Edited by Tanya Gold

www.katherinesilvaauthor.com
www.tanyagold.com

YOU CAN FIND THE ENTIRE COSMOS LURKING
IN ITS LEAST REMARKABLE OBJECTS.

~WISLAWA SZYMBORSKA

There was a good chance that on a particularly gorgeous August day, I might die. It wouldn't be from anything heroic, adventurous, or catastrophic. Heart failure would likely do me in; that or the inability to catch my breath in the tiny solicitor's office in Fulham.

The entire business went on for far too long. There we were, the three of us, sitting outside the office of my father's attorney. Trask, I think his name was or perhaps Traps? Whatever it was, he took his bloody time sorting out the details of this god forsaken inheritance. I'd had nothing to do with my father for the last five years and after this meeting, I hoped to continue in that manner.

We each went in, one after another to speak with the solicitor. The older grumbling chap in his tweed three piece suit that smelled like old texts and cheap liquor, had the first meeting. I recognized the withered, one-foot-in-the-grave expression on his face and the Oxford crest on his lapel. Somehow associated with my father's research at the university, no doubt. His meeting was the shortest and the loudest and he left with a stiff upper lip, reddened cheeks and an air that could only be described as miffed.

Next to go in was a pale skeleton of a woman whom I didn't recognize. I even began to wonder if she had come to the correct office and felt myself begin to ask at one point. My father was one of those misogynistic types. Sure, he'd had a wife, my mother…and he'd dropped her as though she were a hot kettle shortly after I was born. My father hadn't time for women; it was all about the research. That was his one and only passion.

The woman was with the solicitor for nearly twenty minutes and when she left, she carried with her a bound black book and several file folders all held close to her chest.

Then, it was my turn. As I entered and shut the solid mahogany door behind me, I wondered if I, too, would leave the office in a similar disposition to the Oxford fellow. I hadn't expected anything. Father had cut off my allowance when we had parted ways years ago. I figured he would have kept me out of his will as a matter of further penance.

The solicitor waved for me to sit and I did so, awaiting news of empty forbearances. He read from the will, his worm of a moustache wriggling ever so slightly. Millions. I can recall the exact number now but at the time, it was a jumble of digits that left me feeling like crickets were leaping about in my stomach. Not only that; I'd also inherited the deeds for the great

Dawson family estate at Rush End and my father's estate in the United States.

There was a heap of paperwork to sign, for which we made a follow up appointment. I was too stunned to even remember what date we set it for. As I left, it was with a kind of pleased sickness, one that gradually overcame me. I couldn't help but think of how this money was going to be a blessing for me and my family but in the same way, it also terrified me. After all, look what it had done to my father? Would it do the same to us?

The sun seemed too bright outside, the air muggy, and the noises sharp in my ears. All I could smell was the shoe polish from a shiner's stand at the corner. I started for that corner to hail a taxi, turning over and over in my head how I was going to tell my wife about my father's change of heart.

Someone barked something from my distant right. I glanced over to see that Oxford man pointing his finger at the black-clothed woman who had made out better than he had from my father's will.

She stared at him, but I could read nothing in her expression: no surprise, no irritation…nothing. She was turned toward the curb, also hailing a taxi, and barely seemed to register his shouting.

He kept yelling at her and though I couldn't quite tell what he was saying, I saw he was getting angrier as she ignored him, his face getting redder and redder. But I also noted that she hugged the black book closer to her chest the more he said.

For a few moments, I wondered if perhaps I should interject. The man was making quite the scene, others having stopped to stare on their ways up and down the sidewalk. But these two also seemed to know one another beyond the solicitor's office. This argument could have been about a matter entirely devoid of their inheritances from my father and I had no place in that if it was.

A cab pulled up to the curb in front of me. Toying with the thought of getting inside and leaving the dispute behind me, I waved the driver on. The way that woman held the book to her made me think she was trying to protect it from this older man. I waited where I was to see what would transpire.

The taxi I'd let go stopped for the lady. As the driver came running around the car to open the door for her, I heard the Oxford man shout, "Thieving wench!"

The woman disappeared inside the car and soon enough, the cab was zipping down the street into the afternoon haze.

I gazed back to the grumbling older fellow as he stalked down the road toward a shiny black Bentley waiting for him outside of the Italian bakery.

I felt as though everything had been turned upside down that morning and I was suddenly not sure of anything that had happened. Gone were the fears about how to manage the sum of money my father had left me, gone the anticipation of telling my wife about it all…Now, all I could see was that secretive book clutched in the woman's white hands. How could she have stolen it if my father had willed it to her?

I stepped back into the solicitor's, walked past the receptionist's desk and into Trask's office without knocking. He was in the midst of a smoke which he promptly spit out at my entry.

"Who was that woman?" I asked.

"W-what woman?" He juggled the hot cigarette in his hands for a couple moments before dropping it in the ashtray nearby.

I rolled my eyes. "The one that was just here collecting an inheritance from my father."

"I'm sorry, but Miss Rapp asked her identity be…" He trailed off and his face soured with realization.

"Miss Rapp?" The name was unfamiliar to me. "What's her first name?"

Trask straightened in his chair and shook his head. "That's attorney-client privilege. I'm sorry, Mr. Dawson."

I threaded my hands as I sat in the chair before him. "My father trusted you, Mr. Trask. I understand he met with you often."

Trask's eyes slid to the floor. "He did. He was an…interesting client, your father. He desired that his research be left in good hands should the unthinkable happen."

I sighed. "The 'unthinkable' being a fire to destroy not only his office but also himself."

"Nevertheless," Trask's gaze returned to mine, "Professor Dawson wanted discretion."

"And my father paid you quite a bit for it. His fees to you for necessary, some unnecessary visits…I'm sure they helped boost your office's notoriety quite a bit." I nodded to his desk. "Is this mahogany?"

He nervously chuckled.

"Your secretary; couldn't help but notice the perfume. Gardenia? Same as that bottle on the corner of your desk."

Trask snatched the decanter and tucked it into a desk drawer.

I crossed my arms. "Won't the misses be upset?"

Coughing, Trask leaned in. "Right then. It's Inga. Inga Rapp."

A small smile warmed my face. "And what exactly did she inherit from my father?"

"A book."

"As I saw. What sort of book?"

"I don't know. I was told never to look," his eyes got larger. "I didn't, thank you very much."

I scratched my chin. "Something to do with my father's research perhaps?"

Trask shook his head. "I've just told you: I'm not sure."

"Where can I find Miss Rapp? Do you have an address or a telephone number for her?"

"Certainly not," he bristled.

I glanced over my shoulder toward the receptionist. "Seems like a lovely girl. Must be still living at home, I'd think. I wonder, do mum and dad know you've bought her that perfume?"

"You can threaten all you like, Mr. Dawson, but you'll be wasting your time. I never received an address for Miss Rapp; in fact, I have no contact information whatsoever."

I frowned. "How is that possible? You had to be able to contact her about today's appointment."

"I never did. She contacted me via telephone following your father's death. Since I'd already set a date to appoint executors to your father's will and I knew she was named, I scheduled with her then."

"Curious," I mumbled. "How did she know she was listed?"

"Must have been someone important to him, I imagine," Trask said, shrugging.

The statement hit me with the force of a bullet. I stood and turned on my heel. "Good day."

"Remember!" he called after me. "We're signing papers next Tuesday!"

In the cab on the way home, my hands clenched into fists. I wanted to know why she, this Inga Rapp and not one of my father's cohorts from the university was bestowed such a mysterious token of my father's legacy and if it had to do with the illicit reasons I suspected. However much I wanted to believe they hadn't been entangled in an affair, I couldn't keep myself from thoughts of it.

I closed my eyes and tried to enjoy the smell of the summer air, the unfiltered rumble of the motor before me, and feeling of the leather seat under my hands. I had to think about what was ahead of me now, what was ahead for my family. I took a deep breath and let my eyes follow the people and places as they passed by, distracting myself from my feelings about Rapp and making the idea of explaining my inheritance to my wife somewhat easier to swallow.

I chose a more modest life than my father's as an editor with a home in St. John's Wood. It was brick terraced housing and nothing short of ordinary. My son, Emil, kept things interesting for Frances, and me. At four years old, he was still such a small thing with clear blue eyes that always watched me in a questioning way. I spied him from the second story window as the taxi dropped me off in front of the house. He vanished with a swish of the curtains as I started up the walk.

"Peter?" Frances called from the kitchen as I came in and closed the door behind me.

"It's me," I said, shedding my blazer immediately.

Emil bounded into the room and pounced at my legs.

"Hello, Mousey!" I scooped him up in my arms and returned the hug as he squirmed, eager to once again be free.

Frances appeared in the kitchen door, a disapproving look in her eyes but a simper on her lips. "You know I can't stand when you call him that."

I laughed, swinging him around. "Perhaps if he didn't crawl around on the floor so much, it wouldn't be so automatic."

"Oh, well, I suppose we'll have to rename him."

"I think we could settle on a mixture of the two, something like Mousemil? What do you think?" I dipped him upside down and he shrieked with laughter.

"You two." She chuckled and disappeared back into the kitchen. "Dinner will be ready soon. You'd best wash up."

I set Emil down and he raced off into the other room.

Following Frances, I stood in the doorway and watched her stir a pot on the stove, the steam mingling with her chocolate curls. Frances was a fixture in my life as solid as an ash tree, rooted deep in all I did and all I wanted. She had been ever since I'd returned from the war and through the tumultuous severance of my father's and my relationship.

Frances had met my father five years ago in the spring. He had cut off social contact from most everyone he knew and didn't leave the university unless it was to meet with his investments advisor in London or Trask. Getting him to come out for dinner to meet my fiancée was like trying to lure a fox from his hole. He'd finally acquiesced on the condition that we speak alone afterward.

His opinion of Frances was much like his opinion of treacle tart; too sweet, too light, and not good for you. I sat there trembling; every bit of me wanted to knock him off his chair. Frances held my arm and whispered for me not to make a scene. We walked out on a three-course dinner at the Criterion. Whatever private conversation he'd wanted to have never happened. I severed all communication soon after.

Frances and I wed as quickly as we could manage, and purchased our own flat instead of dwelling at Rush End. My father continued to live alone, curling slowly into himself like a withering vine denied water and light.

Water boiling on the stove pulled me back to the present; back to the here and now to the woman I'd chosen to marry.

I came up behind Frances and leaned in to kiss her on the cheek. She smelled of rosemary and soap.

"You seem tired," she noted, and leaned back into my chest.

I held her, arms clasped at her torso. "Speak for yourself. Look at you! You've practically fallen over."

She chuckled while her finger tickled the back of my hand. "Your son decided he wanted to empty all the cupboards today, twice. I spent hours putting things back where they belonged."

I chuckled. "On the bright side, you now know exactly where everything is."

"He found your tobacco, Peter."

I cringed. "So, that's where I put it."

Frances turned around. Her brown eyes had lost some of their mirth. "I know you like a puff every once in a while. It calms you; that I understand. But this is our son! If I hadn't seen him with the box, who knows what he might have done with it..." Her voice trailed off.

"I know. I know," I said, waving my hand. "I forgot about it being there."

Her gaze seemed to go straight through me. "You know you're not at war anymore. You're safe here."

I scoffed. "Of course I know that. You know the saying: Old habits and all that."

"You were calling out in your sleep last night. Did you realize?"

I didn't. My dreams were like smudges of ash on my memory in the morning, painful reminders of the viciousness I'd survived. Now, those nightmares mingled with what I remembered of my father, becoming a welded landscape of devastation and anguish.

Frances looked down at the floor. "I think you should speak to someone. What about Aaron?"

I shook my head. "Not with all he's going through right now with Molly. It's going to be tense enough at the cricket match tomorrow. I don't need to bring any of my own troubles into theirs."

"How about a doctor, then? Molly told me about a publication by that doctor? Freud? It's about war neuroses. Perhaps—"

"Please," I said, taking a step back and shaking my head. "Can we not talk about this right now?"

Frances swallowed and I almost felt the heat of her frustration across the space between us. In spite of the dismay in her eyes, she nodded and whispered, "All right."

Not wanting to end the topic on a sour note, I said, "I promise I'll keep my tobacco in a better place."

Choosing to ignore my answer, she guided me to the kitchen table and we sat there. Her eyes held the same concern she'd had when I'd left that morning. "So," she said, "how did everything go with the solicitor?"

I told her. Rush End, where my father rarely slept after my mother's death, interested Frances as little as it had me. It held nothing but the taste of bad memories. The American property, Hiraeth House, was a more intriguing prospect. I'd visited once in my youth, and the allure and excitement of a new continent made the memories of my limited time there seem idyllic.

Once I'd found a buyer for Rush End, I had it in mind that we'd move to America.

As we ended the conversation and Frances began taking up dinner, I found my thoughts wandering back to that blasted black book once more. As much as I wished I didn't care about my father and his company, I found myself lying awake that night, thinking of them both. What could have been so important that he'd kept it in a silly book—in the care of a woman I'd never met or heard of?

I slept eventually and dreamed. I was a boy again and the leaves were gold and orange. Autumn breezes tugged at my clothes as I ran down the undulating hills of Rush End. If I ran fast enough, the wind would carry me to the ocean, toward white caps and cold salty air. I turned around, looking to see home, looking to see the kind, proud faces of my parents.

Instead, the trees were bare and the house had assumed a blackness and gloom, one that reminded me of the trenches that had become my home while on the front. Silence drowned out everything.

*

The next day, I told Frances that I'd meet her at Aaron's cricket match later that afternoon. "Tell them I wouldn't miss it," I said, snatching my hat from the hook by the door. "I've got a little more paperwork to finish at the office."

She shook her head as she walked into the kitchen. "I wish you didn't have to work so last minute."

"Blasted deadlines."

The words felt heavy as they left my tongue. I felt awful lying to Frances about where I was really going, but it was too late to reveal my true destination. I'd left out the whole matter involving Rapp at the solicitor's office while speaking with her yesterday, mostly because she would read the frustration in my tone.

Frances recognized that the relationship between my father and I was a sensitive one, and even though I tried not to let it get to me, it would. In the days since I'd found out about his death, my nightmares had edged back into my sleep. I knew she saw a correlation between them and would do everything in her power to ensure they didn't overwhelm me, as they had when I first returned from the war.

"Please get to the game before it's over!" she called to me.

"I will." I opened the door and started out.

"Peter!"

I stepped back in. "What?"

"Your briefcase," Frances said, appearing with it in her hand from the den. "You left it by the coffee table."

I swallowed. "Right. I'll need that if I'm to get anything done, won't I?"

She handed it to me and kissed my cheek. "See you later."

I took a cab past my office, past the parks and shops that were familiar to my everyday commute. At King's Cross Station, I found the closest telephone booth and asked the operator to call one of my father's fellow department heads at Hertford College of Oxford. Thurman had worked there about the same length of time as my father and in close concert on several of this research projects. Despite a similar gruffness and disposition, Thurman also was a third cousin of Frances's father and had even come to our wedding.

Thurman picked up the line with his characteristic grouse of being bothered. After we'd said our hellos, I asked if he remembered a particular research partner that my father might have had, a woman with black hair and a reserved demeanor who went by the name Rapp.

He had. What's more: he knew where she spent much of her off time. Rapp had worked with the college often as a visiting scholar and spent much time in the Hertford library trying to set up an exchange program with the library in her hometown of King's Lynn. She was known to practically take up residence there on Saturdays, often with a stack of books "borrowed" from Hertford. Apparently, the exchange program didn't take off.

I thanked Thurman for his time and once I was off the phone, I purchased a ticket to King's Lynn. It was nearly a two hour ride and I wondered on and off if I had a chance of making it back to the match on time at all. All I could think about was that book that Rapp had held, the way she'd cradled it as though it were something to cherish and protect. And the more I thought of it, the more it wound around my brain like twine.

Had she loved my father? Had their relationship been purely platonic, driven by science and a shared curiosity to understand? And if so, what was it that had meant so much to the both of them that they had to conceal it, to protect this information from fellow scholars…and from his only son? I had to know. I had to know as soon as possible, lest it drive me mad each and every night from then on out.

Each time I pondered about getting off the train at the next stop, I forced myself to think of Rapp and her murky-as-the-Thames look the previous day. She was the only one that could answer for my father's secrecy. After thirty-five years of enduring his cold and miserable behavior, of tolerating his inclination toward research versus family, I deserved to know what had been so damn important to him.

The blended smell of salt and metal reached me just as the train pulled into King's Lynn. It was a short distance from the train station to the library so, I elected to walk there and take in the sites. I had only been to King's Lynn a couple times during my youth, both times with my mother to visit old friends. Since then, like many places in England during the Great War, buildings had been damaged and the air of innocence and fond memories that I'd once held had been tarnished by it. Blackfriar's Street, where I now walked, had been spared, but I knew streets to the north, where mother's friends lived, hadn't been so lucky.

The King's Lynn library was cold, a welcome relief from the blistering August heat. I couldn't help but feel as though I were alone in a dark cave, as if warmth couldn't pierce the library's brick and mortar exterior. No wonder Rapp spent so much time in a place like this; it matched what little I knew about her personality. Within moments of entering, I saw her standing with her back to me at the circulation desk, arranging books on a shelf. Her colors remained neutral; a grey skirt and jacket both of which seemed too masculine on her lean and practically boyish figure. Her hair was kept tight in a bun, hidden beneath a black hat. When she turned and saw me, her eyes widened.

"What are you doing here?"

I balked. "Well, that's a fine how-do-you-do if I've ever heard one."

Her face pinched even more than I thought humanly possible. "You shouldn't be here."

"Now, wait a minute," I said, taking a breath to calm myself. "You can't expect me to sit idly by and not question your random insertion in my father's will, can you?"

She scoffed, a characteristic that seemed too warm for her. "What you call "random", your father would have called advantageous."

"And why is that? Because the contents in that book you inherited are too valuable for anyone else to see? Even his other colleagues from the university?"

Her humor flickered away with my words. She grabbed the leather-bound book from the desk and made to walk around me. "I can't talk about it. You shouldn't have come here."

I blocked her way. "On the street yesterday, that other man called you a thief? Did you take something that wasn't yours?"

She straightened. "Those feckless dolts at Hertford wanted a piece of Kian's opus. They'd heard tales of the things he'd uncovered and collected. They think they're owed something because of mere affiliation."

I frowned. She'd called my father by his first name, something that my mother had barely done out of fear to how he would react. He was always the professor in our home, the great Kian Dawson.

She studied my face a moment and said, "He never talked about his family when we worked together. I just assumed he didn't have one."

"We weren't one of his highest priorities," I grumbled, feeling uncomfortable with the statement. "How long did you two work together?"

Her posture relaxed some. "Nearly twenty-seven years, on and off. When he wasn't travelling, we spent much time at the estate cataloguing the collection."

My muscles tensed a moment. "I don't ever remember seeing you around Rush End."

"I never had the pleasure."

"Then what estate did you two work at?"

She shook her head. "I must be going. I have a prior engagement I'm late for."

I squinted. "What kind of collection did you two catalogue and research?"

Looking behind her, she grabbed her purse from the chair at the desk. "You shouldn't ask these kinds of questions," she answered as she slung it over her shoulder. "You won't understand."

"Don't patronize me; I can handle whatever it is."

Rapp took a shaky breath. "It's dangerous and its best if you forget you ever knew about it."

She tried to escape but again, I stood in her way. "What do you mean 'dangerous'?"

"Please, leave me be."

"Not until you answer my question."

The door creaked open behind us and I spun to observe an overweight gentleman approaching. He had a monocle in one eye, large doughy cheeks and a head as bald as an egg. He looked from me to Rapp and back at me again, fixing me with a glare. "Is there a problem here, Ms. Rapp?" he asked.

She stepped back from me and said, "I'm all right. But Mr. Dawson was just leaving."

I eyed the man, contempt hot in my chest as I turned and stalked past him out the door. Damn it all.

*

The cricket match was wrapping up by the time I arrived. Aaron was at a wicket out on the field, panting, his face reddened in the late morning heat. One of his teammates was stepping up to bat. His team was winning by seven runs and now I felt even guiltier that I'd wasted my morning chasing after Rapp.

I found Frances and Molly together sitting at the front of the field, fanning themselves while deep in conversation. A tension seemed to weigh the air around them and I knew at once they had been discussing Aaron's inevitable search for work. Emil was running around with some other children nearby, laughing and screaming.

I apologized for my tardiness and sat alongside my wife. The look in her eye was hesitant and questioning. I sensed she'd interrogate me later.

At home, Frances confronted me once she'd put Emil down for a nap. "Where were you?"

I sighed. "I got tied up with a story. I lost track of time."

She didn't blink. "No. That's not it, is it?"

Somehow she knew.

I rarely lied to my wife, only if I wanted to protect her or keep her from being disappointed. As much as I wished I had been gifted with a silver tongue, I lied with the capacity of a child caught red-handed every time. I didn't want her to worry, but I could see that keeping this from her would do more harm than good. "No, it's not."

"You are being strange," she said, with a spark of anger in her tone. "Why won't you confide in me? Have I lost your trust?"

"You haven't," I assured her, taking both her hands in mine. "It's about my father. All I wanted to do was keep you and Emil from it."

She pulled her hands free and took a step back. "We've been married for five years yet you still have trouble talking to me."

I realized she wasn't referring to my father; she was speaking about the war, the one part of my life that I didn't want to recall, the one place I'd tried to forget.

Instantly, my defenses switched on again. "This has nothing to do with all that."

"It does though. I can see it." Frances's jaw set. "You told me you went into service to get away from him, that you didn't want him controlling who you became… It's the only thing you've ever mentioned to me about the war."

I looked away, my throat thickened and cheeks tingling. "It can't be the only thing…"

"And now that your father has died…" She trailed off, shaking her head.

"What?" I scoffed. "You think I'm going off the deep end?"

"You make it sound as if I haven't reason to worry." She stepped into me and held my hands, her eyebrows knitted. "But I do worry, Peter. I only want for you to be happy and your father was such an unkind man…"

"There, there…" I put my arms around her. "I had hoped with him gone, I'd be able to leave those memories behind. But all of our time together, the good and the bad, seems to have risen to the surface that much quicker."

Her eyes softened. "You do miss him, don't you?"

I shook my head hastily. "No. I really don't."

"He was nasty. And cruel," she agreed, lifting my chin with her hand. "But he was your father."

He was in the sense that we shared the same blood and name. Frances didn't understand. In her eyes, a father was always a father and no matter the relationship you shared, you permanently harbored some essence of love for him. Such was not the case with me and mine.

But I needed to let this go. It was going to poison my life unless I pried my fingers from it. He was gone. No use in dwelling on the things that couldn't be changed. So, I kissed Frances's hair and said, "Forgive me. He won't be trouble for us anymore."

*

That night as I lay in bed, Frances sound asleep beside me, my mind plunged into the memories of my youth.

Rapp's words about this so-called "collection" of my father's made me think of the weeks he'd spent abroad, exploring the dark jungles in El Salvador, Mesopotamian ruins in the Ottoman Empire, and the sands of Egypt. I never knew what he did on these excursions, and my curiosity about them was often rewarded with irritation and an insistence that they were to dreary scientific lectures. My father was always so much more displeased at home in the times between these trips.

I imagined he spent days sitting in stuffy rooms listening to others prattle on about the driest of methodical inquiries and soon, I grew less and less interested in where he went just as long as he went. My father was absent for a great portion of my childhood, which is probably the reason I found those times without him not lonely but tranquil.

Not every moment with him was so horrible. That night, I chose to seek out the times my father had dealt me a kind word or respect. I thought of the time he gifted me a bicycle and taught me to ride it though I was a slow learner. I remembered when he and I had spent a couple afternoons fishing by the river at Rush End, neither of us speaking a word, content in our silence. When I graduated from Sheffield University, he had actually shown up and appeared proud. I'd overheard him more than once talking to his peers that I was "his father's son". At the time, that statement made me more ill than grateful.

These remembrances were few and far between the odious ones and instead of being comforted by them, I only felt more chafed. That inquisitiveness I thought I had lost about those long tours he used to take came back to me tenfold. I never thought of my father as a collector, more a kind of obsessive observer. But if what Rapp said was true, did it mean there things he'd kept secret for the sake of research, hidden away in some estate somewhere?

I had lied to Frances and myself when I'd said I could let the past go. I still couldn't escape my father, even after his death. There were too many things still unanswered.

*

On Monday, I attempted to carry on with my normal existence and returned to work at the Downing Post. I spent a few hours sitting in my office editing stories as was my daily routine. Soon enough though, I was staring off into space, chewing on a pencil absentmindedly as I thought about Rapp and the book again. That spider of a woman and the things she wouldn't say about that collection had clawed her way into my mind so deeply, I couldn't focus on much of anything.

I asked my secretary, Rowena, to put in a call to the King's Lynn Town Hall under the ruse that it was for a story. Once she connected me, I asked if the receptionist there could check on any property owned by Rapp or my father. If Rapp wasn't going to tell me where this estate was, I'd have to find out for myself.

The receptionist's nasal voice whined in my ear that it would take her several hours to find the necessary information. She deigned that she'd call back when she knew, and promptly hung up.

It was afternoon before she returned my call. I'd edited only two stories in the meantime, having very little willpower to focus on them. She reported that my father had purchased a parcel of land north of King's Lynn, somewhere in the woods above Castle Rising and south of Wolferton.

I didn't understand. There was practically nothing out there. What did Rapp so desperately want to protect?

I left work before five, much to the chagrin of my editor-in-chief who was dead-set on making me read a colleague's story about a bad milk poisoning. I told him I thought I'd had some of that milk myself and feigned sickness all the way out the door.

I thought about taking Tuesday to investigate the property and returned home to spend more time going over my father's investments, things that actually required my time and energy.

I tried to hail a cab but the way I'd normally travel home was blocked by throngs of people in the road. Apparently, there was a non-violent demonstration of some kind. I could hear someone shouting above a low hum of conversation and the distant sounds of police horns coming to break it up. I decided to walk; after all, it wasn't far to St. John's Wood. I followed Whitehall to the roundabout and Trafalgar Square.

I neared Nelson's Column, spiring into the sky like a needle. One of the lion statues at the base faced me, head erect, stone mane like liquid bronze in the lowering light. My chest tightened. My legs stiffened like rusted iron, every step felt like a challenge to perform. I forced my eyes to close, if only for a moment, and in the darkness, I could see the lions springing for me, claws slicing the air.

I bolted, nearly running into a couple blokes having a smoke. The stench of tobacco filled my lungs as I wildly pushed through them and kept going. I didn't breathe easy until I left the square, my shirt sticking to me and my lungs on fire. No, the lions weren't real, they barely looked it. But closing my eyes had brought back my memories of them as though it were only yesterday.

When Frances and I courted years prior, we'd gone to the London Zoo to see Winnie, the spirited black bear. On our way out, I heard a frightful roar. My heart instantly leapt into my throat as one of the large male lions approached the front of its enclosure licking its chops. I was trapped in its gaze, not trusting the silent way it padded toward us. The fence between us was a joke, a mockery of safety. The lion could spring at any moment, hook me or Frances in its claws before anything could be done about it. Without a word, I yanked her away, practically dragged her, not stopping until we were safely outside the zoo gates.

Late evening was cool. Emil and Frances had already retired to bed and I decided to indulge in a smoke, for it had been several days since my last one. I needed one that evening. I couldn't turn off all the troublesome thoughts about Rapp, the estate, and that lion in Trafalgar Square.

It was a blustery night, the wind strong and whipping. Outside on the front stoop, I'd only had a couple puffs and was just beginning to relax. The streets were practically empty and the only sounds were an owl and the distant voices in the park a few blocks away. Inhaling, I was startled by the clatter clop of heels at an awkward pace coming up the sidewalk toward me. As the figure drew closer, I recognized Inga Rapp's stick-like figure and her usually cold expression tinged by exasperation.

I coughed, smoke pouring from my mouth. "Good God, woman, whatever is the matter?" I said, as she practically stumbled into me.

"Here, take this. Take it!" She frantically shoved a book into my hands. "You must not let them find it. You mustn't let them take it."

I hurriedly pushed the cigarette into my mouth, lest I light the book on fire. "Slow down. What are you talking about?"

"Promise me, you will not enter the estate." Her black eyes seemed to usher doom and dowsed me with dread.

"Tell me what this is all about," I asked but she let go of me and the book with her long nails and continued briskly down the block. The book she'd given me was the very same one she'd tried to keep from me at the library, the one she'd received from the solicitor's office.

I thought about following her. I should have. But I was more irritated and confused than ever. What was worse was that the commotion had awoken Frances and she'd opened the window above.

"What was that racket?" she asked.

I spit out the cigarette and shrugged my shoulders as I tried to stub the butt out with the heel of my shoe. "Drunks."

*

Tuesday, I returned to the Downing Post, not wanting to think about last night's encounter with Rapp and so as not to tiptoe around Frances. Even after trying to hide the cigarette, she'd still smelled it on me after I'd come in. She'd made me spend the night on the sofa. I sensed she was still cross with me about our conversation Saturday evening, too. Despite my desire to ignore Rapp's book, I brought it along. I feared

Frances might find it while tidying. Then she'd worry even more.

Unedited reports were stacked on my desk as usual. The top most pages detailed the murder of Ms. Inga Rapp, a spinster librarian, in Trafalgar Square.

I dropped into my chair; my legs felt like pudding as I read the article. It seemed that Rapp was thrown in front of a passing car. While no one was able to identify the person who pushed her, a witness recalled the figure of a tall, gangling man vanishing into the shadows of an alleyway. The constabulary found nothing on her save for a note, what seemed to be an address. I wondered if it had been mine.

I'd been staring at it for minutes before I noticed my office secretary, Rowena, standing in the doorway. "You've barely touched your coffee. Must be a good one you've got there," she said, wiping a blonde bang from out of her eyes. "I'd be happy to type it up for you when you've finished."

In a panic, I tried to push Rapp's book to my left but it met with a stack of papers which toppled to the floor. Leaping out of my chair, I quickly began to sort them. "I'm sorry. I didn't get much sleep last night."

Rowena knelt down to help me. A wave of her gardenia perfume swept over me, and those big blue eyes filled with concern. Lord in heaven, my editor-in-chief hadn't hired the youngest and prettiest girl in the office just for her quick typing.

"It's okay," I said. "I've got it."

"You look as white as a sheet," she continued, "Perhaps you've come down with something."

I quickly stood and dropped the papers on my desk. For moments, I wondered if I was losing my grip on reality, if what I'd read had truly happened. But one more look confirmed it; Rapp was dead and the book she'd handed me was still on the floor like an omen of last night's encounter.

"I'm fine. Really. But I can't have any interruptions today."

Rowena nodded. With brows still furrowed, she left me and closed the door behind her. I picked Rapp's book up from the floor, and without sitting, opened the cover as if something might reach out and snap at me.

In swirling script after a few blank pages, I found the words "The Collection" inscribed followed by author's names, Professor Kian Dawson, and Inga Rapp's in smaller letters below that. At the bottom in all caps read: "MAJORITY HOUSED AT CAULFIELD MANOR". I turned the next page.

A penned sketch of a full-length mirror took up most of the sheet. It looked like a mirror any one would find at a great house, something a lady might stare into while observing her new gown or a gentleman admiring a new jacket. It reminded me much of the one my own mother had. The head of the page was titled "The Hall of Işkence: mirrors recovered and restored from an archaeological dig in Ephesus. Threat: High. Control your fear."

"Control your fear…" I whispered, my voice sounding almost too loud in the silence of my office. What did that even mean?

The next page showed a similar sketch of a suit of armor, although it was not of a design I'd ever seen. "The Paladin: found in the Pass of Roncevalles in the Spanish Pyrenees. Threat: High. Silence is necessary."

I stared at the words until they seemed to blur together.

Silence was "necessary"? "Control" my fear? What did that have to do with anything? And why had my father classified these individual things as though they were…

Rapp's voice returned to me hesitantly. Dangerous.

A knock on my door brought my head up. Rowena pushed in before I could answer. "The Chief is waiting for your final edits on the riot story. I tried to tell him you were busy and he looked like he was about to blow his top…" Her words faded. "Goodness, what is that? Are you okay, Mr. Dawson? You look positively baffled."

Behind her, I noticed several others glancing in my direction. It was as if they, too, could sense the rising stress caused by this book.

"I need to leave," I said. This was not the place for this; not the time. I couldn't concentrate on work while these startling revelations about my father's sanity stared me in the face.

"But, what do I tell—"

"I'll have the edits for him first thing in the morning." I shoved the book into my briefcase. "Cover for me, would you? Attagirl," I said, not waiting for a response as I darted around her and out the front door. I didn't have a plan for where I'd go but, nevertheless, my feet guided me in a direction other than home.

I couldn't go back to the house. No doubt, Frances was still upset with me and I was determined to keep my family separate from all of my father's affairs, as insane as they were. If Rapp's death was connected to this book, I wanted Frances and Emil as far away from danger as possible.

My arrival at King's Cross was an unplanned act. It was as if I was watching myself from the outside, a composed and collected version of myself who seemed to know exactly what he was doing.
I came out of my haze during the train ride. A man asked to join me in my compartment and I stared at him as if he'd just sprung into existence. He mumbled and moved on.

Glancing down at my ticket confirmed that I was on the train to King's Lynn. I stared out at the countryside, the morning light banking against the hills. This couldn't go on any longer. Today, I'd find this Caulfield Manor and uncover this supposed "collection" there.

Undoubtedly, the police would find a witness who would say that Rapp bumped into me outside my house. Or, they'd find I'd gone to see her at the King's Lynn library and that our meeting had been less than amicable. I'd be forced to turn over the book in order to corroborate my story, and that might have still incriminated me.

I looked down at the book once more and felt my stomach turn at the thought of opening it up again. What was written along those pages seemed to be nothing more than absurdity. Dangerous mirrors and suits of armor? Had my father and this equally disturbed woman spent twenty-seven years compiling a list of fantastic objects with the realness of a child's nightmare? Did the actual collection even exist or was it too born of two ill and addled minds?

I wasn't sure if I wanted it to be folly and to think my father crazy or to believe that his and Rapp's deaths had been more than just accidents and that this collection was actually as dangerous as was portended.

A lump grew in my throat. Rapp had made a reference to "them" when she'd given me the book. What if this mysterious "them" were the ones who had killed her trying to get the book? What if these people were still after the book and discovered that I now had it? Would they come looking to kill me as well? Would they go after Frances? Would they hurt Emil?

I started to wish that I'd never gone to work that morning, that I'd never seen that unedited report about her death. All it had done was open the doors to a commotion of horrible probabilities that jumbled about in my head and wouldn't be silenced.

I shook my head and pleaded with myself to think straight. Then again, what if Rapp was batty after all? These people she'd told me were after her… What if they were a product of hysteria and the person who purportedly killed her was a jilted ex-lover or a disgruntled colleague? It might have even been an indiscriminate homicide. Perhaps she'd stepped out in front of that car herself without looking…

I sat, rubbing my knuckles. The little compartment felt hot and cold as I fluctuated between anxiety and then sensible relief. What if I raced all the way back home and found that everything was as it should be? The only way to confirm if this Caulfield Manor was as dangerous as Rapp said was to go and look at the property myself. I needed to be sure; I needed confirmation.

When it came time to switch trains at King's Lynn, I spent a half an hour trying to convince myself to board the Wolferton train, pacing to and fro while I smoking a cigarette down to the stub. Spying a telephone box, I pushed in, deposited a few coins, and asked the operator to connect me with the Pavillion at the Lord's Cricket Ground in St. John's Wood. I prayed Aaron was there as I knew it was rare for him to be home this early in the day. A young man picked up on the other line and I asked him to put Aaron on the phone if he was available. My hands were shaking.

Why was this so hard? Perhaps because I worried that he was at his wit's end with everything.

Finally, Aaron came on the line, laughing and said, "Hello?"

"Aaron, I…" What was I going to say? How was I going to say it? I suddenly couldn't make my mind work. No matter how I put things, he was going to think I was barmy on the crumpet.

"Peter, is that you? Can you repeat that? You've cut out a bit."

"Sorry, I…I just…" What if I told him and unwittingly made him a target as well? It was silly; thinking there was a grand conspiracy surrounding my father. But I couldn't help it. And I certainly didn't want anyone I cared about being in danger because of it.

"What's wrong? Are you all right?" Aaron asked.

I took a deep breath. "I'm getting on a train to Wolferton."

"Wolferton? Why in hell's bells are you—"

"If I don't call you back tonight, promise me you'll phone the police."

"Peter, what are you on about? What's happened?"

I hung up. In some demented way, I felt better. If indeed there were people after Rapp and they managed to find me, I knew police would investigate my disappearance or be suspicious if I turned up dead.

Furthermore, if the nameless sect fixed their sights on Aaron, he wouldn't be complicit in any of this. On the other hand, if the estate turned out to be a complete fluke, I could call him back and explain that I'd had too much to drink or that I was investigating a risky story... I'd come up with something.

When I finally boarded the train, I didn't let my mind wander, if only to keep my calm. I'd done the only thing I could to get myself out of a jam if I found myself in one. I spent the ride drinking an Old Fashioned and staring at the blurring green scenery. I itched for a cigarette, but realized I'd rolled only two that morning and already used one. I convinced myself to keep the last one, in case I needed an emergency smoke later. To distract myself, I ignored the turning of my tummy and read further on into Rapp's book.

There were more objects on each page that seemed to have no correlation to one another but to my father were apparently one-of-a-kind antiques. One page detailed a delivery of taxidermy animals split into two separate freights. There seemed to be extra fervor about a black rhino among the animals transported elsewhere.

Other pages spoke of a chandelier made entirely from human bones, hundreds of gallons of what appeared to be ordinary water from a lake in the Middle East, strange plants harvested from the darkest heart of Africa, and an old piano. The list went on and on. Each page included a brief description of where it had come from followed by a threat level that ranged from low to high and finally a sentence that seemed to make no sense what so ever.

The train took a bend and my insides shifted. We were slowing down. I peered out the carriage window to the track ahead of us. Wolferton Station was a Tudor-style structure with a clay-shingled roof. I'd never been a fan of the architecture; it always made me feel uneasy. The dark wood striped against the white reminded me of a prison cell. There were no passengers waiting on the platform which didn't surprise me. Wolferton mostly catered royal trains and to the Sandringham House, home for the monarchy. Most of the people that rode the lines were either guests of Sandringham or workers transporting supplies to and from the house.

I stepped down onto the platform, my shoes against the worn bricks the only sound, and proceeded into the station. An oak paneled room awaited me inside. Leather easy chairs dotted the room and a great clock chimed the midday hour. Save for the lonely ticket officer, whose wrinkle-deepened face and hooded eyes made me question his efficacy, the station was empty.

"When is the next train scheduled to come through?" I asked him.

"Only one more train departing this station today," he said, his voice congested and eyes still in a drowsed state. I still couldn't quite master the eccentric and somewhat otherworldly dialect that Norfolk sometimes demonstrated. Taking a deep breath, I calmed myself for the muddled tête-à-tête I was sure awaited me with the ticket officer.

"Only one?""

He nodded.

"What time is the next train departing?""

"Round four, I reckon.""

I straightened and checked the clock. Four hours to find my father's estate, investigate, and get back to the train. I had no idea where to even look. The ticket officer was beginning to nod off.

"One more question…""

He perked back up.

"How do I get to Caulfield?""

"About two and a half miles on from here. Take a left out front and follow the road 'til you get the intersection, then follow the southern road.""

"Wait…follow the road? Isn't there a taxi running today?""

" 'fraid not.""

I sighed. "Looks like I'm walking then." I started toward the door to the street and looked back over my shoulder. "I'll be back for that four o'clock train. Don't let it leave without me.""

He nodded and settled down in his seat to resume his nap.

I set off on my path to Caulfield and followed the bending road from civilization into wild, unpredictable greenery. I lost myself in it, remembering the days when I used to explore Rush End in my youth. Everything seemed remarkable then, from the colors of the leaves to the various types of plants. I never grew bored of it, distracted by the thoughts that beyond its ordinary beauty, there was a different world out there from the one I knew, something just out of my reach waiting to be found. My imagination became moribund as I grew up, depleted by my father's own dismissive behavior and my mother's wilting spirit. It had felt like neglecting a bud that had only just begun to bloom.

A dense hedge grew along the roadside for the next mile or so, blocking my view of the forest. The only clarity came from overhead, a pristine blue bowl and clouds that raced by as if trying to escape. The wind had picked up, but was cool and welcome on my perspiring brow. It was another scorcher of a day and my suit might as well have been made of molten lava.

Eventually the hedges dwindled and the road opened into a four way intersection. Lilac blossoms burst from nearly every empty space between the trees and their sweet scent pulled me from the suspicious quietude. I veered right and continued on.

*

The next half an hour was spent admiring the scenery, listening to the chirps of woodcocks and golden orioles, my feet slowly but surely blistering. My shoes were not made for a pilgrimage; they were meant for sitting behind a desk all day. I began to check my pocket watch obsessively, worrying that it was going to take longer than I'd calculated. I probably should have called it off and waited for the return train home. I could have come another day… It was too late now. I'd already walked an hour out of my way. Just get it over and done with it.

The woods thinned and I looked out across a field of lavender toward an imposing structure. It looked as though it might have once belonged to a well-off family, a disused abbey built of sand-colored brick and mortar. Someone might have mistaken it for Sandringham if they didn't know their own way, but I felt something in my stomach, a sort of sickness that confirmed the authenticity and the mystery of my father's estate to me. I wasn't wrong. This was Caulfield.

I traversed the dirt road that wound through the field, the sweet floral scent of lavender a pleasant distraction in the face of Caulfield's cryptic manor. Verdant sheets of ivy drew up around much of the house's front façade, almost like a mask. I dreaded what I might find hidden behind it. Much like with Wolferton Station, I was aware of an undulating discomfort upon looking at this place, one that deepened the closer I came.

The estate was impressive, though neglected. Gnarled hedges blocked my view beyond the front while a great brick wall with gated arches stood between me and Caulfield. Once I reached the gates, I curled my fingers around the iron bars and stared past them. No curtains were drawn but the inside of the house appeared black and cold. I doubted my father kept any staff there and couldn't imagine who else could be around. Then, I didn't want to think who might be.

I leaned on the gate and was surprised when it creaked open. A rusted lock plopped into the stones at my feet. With all the secrecy surrounding the estate and Rapp's fear of anyone finding out about it, I imagined things would have been better secured. Still, I was glad I didn't have to scale what appeared to have been an insurmountable wall. My shoes sank in the crushed pebbles as I crossed to the front door and struck the knocker.

The sound echoed against a vast and empty space on the other side. I took a step back, smoothed my hair, and pulled the creases from my suit. I didn't care how I looked; I had to find something to do with my hands other than wring them obsessively. After a minute, I struck again. No one came to the door. No one was there. Against all of my better judgement, I thumbed down the latch and pushed on the door. It wouldn't budge.

Should have figured it'd be locked. Perhaps there was a key somewhere. Had the key been with Rapp when she was killed? Either the police or the people after the book could have it by now if that was the case. Perhaps there was a spare, one nearby in case the original got lost… I opened the book once more, and carefully flipped through the first few pages once again.

Beneath the Damask, you'll find a skeleton.

It was half way down one of the pages I'd thought was blank in the tiniest handwriting, and didn't seem to correspond to anything else mentioned about the house. But I knew my father's hand; I knew his penchant for speaking in half-truths and riddles. The skeleton was likely a skeleton key; the Damask…?

My gaze settled on an untamed rose bush to the right of the door, full of burgeoning pale pink roses. Several had wilted in the extreme heat, while the ones nestled deepest within the leaves and thorns thrived.

Damask roses. They were one of my mother's favorites.

Laying the book and my jacket on the front step, I crouched down by the rose bush and pawed at the soil around it. Bugger it all. I hadn't gotten close enough. I reached my hand further underneath the spikey tendrils and pushed my fingers into the dirt once again. It was an awkward angle, my other hand aching as I balanced on it to keep me from falling flat on my face. Finally, my nails scratched against a smooth cold box. I wrenched it from the soil bed in one go, thorns snagging against my hand as I brought it into the light.

"Ah!" I dropped the box onto the grass and looked at the damage. Drops of blood rolled down the backside of my hand. I plucked a rag from my coat pocket on the step and dabbed at them, leaving pale red streaks across the white cotton. Retrieving the box from where I'd dropped it, I lifted the lid to see a tiny bundle of red cloth. Wrapped inside was a skeleton key. Discarding the cloth and collecting my things from the step, I slipped the key into the lock and turned it. The click made my breath falter and against all better judgement, I pushed in the door.

The front hall scowled at me as a sliver of light from the entrance revealed its grandeur. The high ceilings depicted rose-copper scenes of war. Frescos of blackened earth and bleached sky seemed to depict the collision of heaven and hell in the arches above the doors that lined each side of the hall.

My feet moved on their own accord. After a few steps, the front door slammed and blackness folded down around me. I jumped, my heartrate fluttering as I listening to the roughness of my own breath. Two lanterns on opposite sides of the hall came to life and their faint light flickered the room back into existence.

I couldn't make myself turn around. Every shadow seemed ominous; every creak I heard a prelude to death. Someone was here, playing games with me. Perhaps Rapp was right to be afraid. Perhaps her killer had found this place before I could…

Steady on, I thought to myself and relaxed my shoulders which had stiffened without my permission. You need answers!

The smallest part of me, the most hated part of me wanted, no, needed to know more. There were doors all around me that would presumably take me to some of the things my father had collected. The part of me that longed for fantasy, that I thought had suffocated in my childhood needed to be placated. This was the brink of my imagination's reawakening and its ultimate demise. I wasn't ready to walk away yet. I didn't want to be a severe and skeptical father as my own had been to me. It was hard for me to even imagine my father had believed in all of this after how he'd treated me as a boy.

"A child's reverie is much like this fungi," he'd once told me as he plucked a mushroom from the grass back home. "It is only necessary to a certain set of artistic individuals. Here in this house, it is merely a blemish on a manicured lawn." He flung it toward the wood's edge. "Best you not let it flourish on your mind."

I didn't want to be the reason my own son lost his sense of wonder.

I pressed on. The decision before me now was simple: which room to enter. There were no marks on the book pages that suggested where each item was. It was a guessing game and if what the book suggested was true, there could be a threat of death in any one of them. I decided on a whim to enter the door at the end of the hall, in hopes that I could eventually see the grounds hidden behind the overgrown hedges. Holding the book close to me, I opened the impeccable mahogany door and entered.

I may as well have stepped into another realm. Thick mustard yellow tapestries hung across the walls like a strange sinew. Ghastly artwork of skeletal figures framed by brambles hung on either side of an ebony dining table. It stretched down the narrow room, a tray at its center where a hunk of something sat alone.

The door clicked closed behind me. I tried the handle but it wouldn't budge. Somehow, it had locked from the other side.

I willed myself to awaken, to once again see the passing landscape in my train car. This isn't real. I'm not really here.

The soft screech of a chair made me open my eyes. Nothing moved save for the flicker of candlelight at each corner of the room.

Then, I noticed him. Seated at the head of the table was a knight. I don't understand how I missed him for he was easily the most terrifying thing before me. Instead of armor, his shoulders were cloaked by bristly shards of bone, some that grew from its decayed figure. Skin had rotted away to reveal ropey muscles along his arms and taut abdominals. A husk of bone encircled his neck and the remains of a smooth helmet left only one opening at his toothily gaped mouth. Horns jutted from its crown like antlers.

He sat erect with his arms at his sides, one hand clutching a carved staff with a long spearhead that gleamed under the low light.

My heart was in my throat. I waited for this demon to rise, to come for me, to thrust the spear into my chest. The figure didn't move, didn't look as though it could sustain life, not in such a wasted condition.

I stepped forward and held my breath. The creature stayed still.

The train ride had fatigued me. The book and Rapp's lingering warning kept me on edge. The creature at the end of the table was merely someone's keen idea (my father's apparently) of a practical joke. What had he called it in his book? The Paladin. I recognized the crude sketch I'd seen. Monstrous! I never wanted to sleep again for fear it would prey on me in the night. In that instant, I realized that my father had elicited a weakness from me without being alive to do so and it made me all the more exasperated.

Gradually, I made my way across the room, my eyes never leaving the Paladin. I'm not sure why I'd drawn the comparison of him to a knight. Harkening back to my childhood readings about King Arthur and his knights of the round table, I knew they were perceived as being symbols of chivalry, honor, and bravery. This creature looked as though it had been raised from the depths of Hell. Whatever or whoever he had been when he was alive could not have been regarded so highly, I decided.

Midway across the room, I gagged. I could finally see what was on the platter in the center of the table. A hunk of red raw flesh oozed over the lip of the silver tray and onto the table's surface. Blood drained from my face as I backed away and bumped into the wall.

The Paladin swiftly stood from his chair.

I froze. Blood roared in my ears and my pulse thumped in my neck.

He didn't move any further, had once again become like stone; rigid and motionless. What was he doing? Why didn't he come at me?

I suddenly remembered the page devoted to the Paladin in the book and the line my father scribbled in that hadn't made any sense to me. "Silence is necessary."

He had heard me. Now that I was perfectly still and not making sounds, he couldn't. As long as I didn't make any noise, he couldn't move.

The Paladin stood between me and the door, ten feet away. If I was going to get out of here, I needed to pass within inches of him and be completely silent.

I swallowed the fear that threatened to gallop from me and took a small step away from the wall. The Paladin remained where he was. I inched my way along the edge of the room. My eyes flicked back and forth between my own feet and the Paladin's. He hadn't turned to follow my movements.

I was close enough to see the rough texture of his spikes, the desiccation of his skin, the hollow grooves and crags on his body beneath the horrific armor. Could he sense my nervous breathing? I held it.

The door was only a couple feet from me. Just a little further... I thought as I lifted my foot and took another step. He still hadn't moved. I was almost there. A little more...

A floorboard squeaked.

The Paladin swung his spear at me. I ducked to the right in time for it to whoosh past my ear. Stumbling, I scrabbled for the door. The rattle of bone and pop of joints moved behind me. I wrenched the door open, a dreadful pressure on my back. He's so close. He's going to—

Fingers snagged on my jacket as I tried to escape. I flung it from my shoulders, pulling my arms free as it was torn from me. Barreling through the door, I shouldered it shut.

Bang! Something slammed against the other side and my arm ignited with pain. I backed away, holding it as blood raced down my white shirtsleeve. The spear tip jutted through the solid mahogany. I backed away, waiting for the Paladin to open the door and come at me.

Nothing. He couldn't hear me. He couldn't move anymore.

Swallowing air as though it was quenching a thirst, I backed as far away as I could manage. I'd nearly died in there! What the hell kind of collection had my father assembled? What reason did he have for putting that thing in a room? Hell, how had he even gotten it in there without being skewered alive?

I felt flush. I tugged at my collar and winced, almost forgetting about my arm. It was still bleeding. Rolling up my sleeve confirmed it was nothing more than a surface scratch, though it could have been much, much worse. What if he'd hit me in the chest? Or the head?

The warmth was almost unbearable. I soon realized I stood in a sunbeam that coursed through the window at my left. I ran to it, and gawked at the world outside. I didn't care anymore about father's secrets nor Rapp's obsessions; none of it mattered. All I wanted was get out of that house and get back to the train before it left. But I wasn't going back through that hellish dining room. I'd have to find another way out of the house.

My fingers pried at the window, trying to lift it but it wouldn't budge. It was sealed shut. I scanned the room for something to break the glass with. I was in a library, the walls completely covered with rows and rows of books. I slid a thick tome out from a shelf and scanned the title: Collected Texts on Vigor in Art.

How positively dull. I lobbed the book at the window as hard as I could. It bounced off and splattered to the floor.

The clunk of something at the door made me whip around. The spearhead was now gone.

Damn it… If I smashed the glass and the Paladin heard it, he might come through that door. I'd need to hurry out that window.

There was nothing heavier in the room I could use to bust the glass; no stone or metal bookends, no chairs, no lamps. Out of the corner of my eye, I spied a standing globe. The sphere was dark navy and speckled with dots that marked countries, and cross-hatched by longitude and latitude lines. My father had had one like it in his personal study. The few times I was allowed inside, I used to spin it and let my finger stop in a random place upon it. Then, I'd find one of his books and look at all the information I could about that particular place. It was a silly game I played with myself, and in a strange way, I missed the whimsy of it.

I brushed my fingers over the globe and gave it a slight turn.

The floor dropped out from beneath my feet. I seized the globe stand as the entire room folded over. The thunderous roar of revolving plaster and wood drowned out my own cries of terror. I lost my grip on my father's book and it fell toward the window now directly below me. Then, the rest of them came. Books rained from the shelves above me, the thick volumes thundering down on my fingers and my head. The glass in the windows cracked with each pound against them and finally shattered. Disturbed and terrified, I forced myself to hold on through the literary storm until the last of the books had tumbled and only silence pervaded.

I dangled from the globe stand, the only thing bolted to the floor in the upended space. Sweat trickled down my brow and my injured arm ached. If I fell, I'd likely go through the shattered window and cut myself up, perhaps fatally, in the process. I peered at the globe.

I stretched my hand out and swished it through the air, my body teetering back and forth with the failed attempt to reach the globe. I wasn't close enough. Curling my clammy hands further around the globe stand, I shimmied as close as I could. Every time I happened to look down, my stomach pivoted much like the room had. Reaching out once more, I finally touched the globe and a prick of hope returned to me. As I carefully glided Europe back down toward me, the hand anchoring me slipped.

I hurtled toward the window, my surroundings a blur. Unexpectedly striking the carpet, I rolled to a stop against a pile of books beneath the broken window. The room tilted at an angle and rocked back and forth in time with the globe. Shaking, I climbed the sloping floor to the orb before steering the earth back to where it belonged.

The world was once again how it ought to be. The floor was once again flat beneath my feet, the walls at either side of me.

I collapsed to my knees and retched. For a few minutes, it was hard to get my bearings, to tell which way was up and down. My mind raced. I had to get out of here. I needed to.

Light glinted on the broken glass in the window. The warmth of the sunlight helped me gather my senses. I wiped my mouth and got to my feet. I now had a way out of the house.

I spent a few minutes sifting through the piles of books, searching for the book Rapp had given me. Part of me hoped I wouldn't find it, that it had miraculously vanished in the flurry that the globe had caused. Alas, I spotted the cordovan cover peeking out. For moments, I considered leaving it behind. Taking it with me was almost like committing myself to remembering this horror. But I knew that should the police come to me during their investigation of Rapp's death, I'd need it as proof of what she was involved in. I tucked it under my arm before I left.

I cleared the rest of the hazardous glass shards in the window easily using the book. All through it, I kept my eyes on the Paladin's door. Perhaps his room was upended, too, and he now lay on the floor like a turtle that couldn't right itself. I smirked as the thought provided me with an odd sort of comfort.

I crawled through the window and leapt down into a soft bed of green. The flawless sky welcomed me and I drew in lungfuls of sweet-smelling air as if I hadn't tasted it in years. The horizon line burned saffron and orange signaling the decent into evening. I needed to get back to the train before it left. I glanced around for a way back to the road.

Dense evergreen hedges rose up around me and blocked my way to the front of the house. Needles jabbed at my arms and the cut branches scraped my chest as I tried to squeeze through them, but there was not enough room. Thorns had grown in amongst the yew, making them impossible to climb without ripping myself to shreds.

"Hello! Anyone!" I called out. Someone had to hear. But the house was a half mile from the road and I doubted anyone could hear me from so far away.

The only open path was a brick walkway to my direct right, leading to the back of the house. Steeling myself, I followed it.

Twisting in and around vegetation, I followed the trail through shadows where tufts of ostrich ferns flourished and candelabra primroses popped like roman candles. After a few minutes, I came to a clearing where a magnificent greenhouse stood. Every wall was made of glass and revealed an impressive array of fronds inside. Delicate branches of orchids, tendrils of morning glory, and starburst swords of gladiolus peeked out, bursts of color within a green world. White tulips lined the front walk to its entrance. It was the first thing about Caulfield Manor that I could call beautiful, the only thing that had made me feel at ease since I'd arrived.

Yet, that apprehensive feeling in my stomach couldn't be quelled.

Beyond the greenhouse, there appeared to be another path that wound back toward the manor through the bushes and trees. The quiet put me on edge. I felt very uneasy out in the open, as if something unseen and ominous lurked in the pure beauty of that sky I'd found so refreshing moments ago.

I unlatched the door to the greenhouse and stepped inside. Warm moisture surrounded me, dampening my clothes and hair. Slivers of sunlight cut through the foliage and dispersed in the haze. Brushing leaves aside, I inched my way toward the opposite end of the greenhouse.

Rapp was right to be paranoid. To think this place and these things not only existed but were the target of someone who wanted them for an unknown purpose... I couldn't fathom why my own father had wanted them.

Even as I began to further doubt his mental stability, I realized there was a perfectly legitimate reason for it all. My father would have studied the items; it was why he locked himself away in his last years, why he had seemed to have lost his mind. Anyone else who'd come across globes that upended rooms, or desiccated murderous corpses that came to life at the smallest sound probably would have lost their mind. But my father's obsessive curiosity knew no bounds when it came to his work and his nature called for him to research. Like most things he studied, this study became a fixation. Did he know there were people out there who wanted these items so badly and were willing to kill to get them? If so, it might have explained his fanatical temperament all the more.

As I stopped to wipe the dew and perspiration from my brow, my shoulders prickled as if spiders crawled across my skin. I felt as if I were being watched, my every move dissected. I investigated the ferns until my eyes rested on another set of eyes. These were the color of whisky and there was something in them that was animated, yet somehow inert. I waited to see recognition, a sudden rustling before whatever they belonged to sprung from their cover. It never happened.

Carefully peeling back the fronds, I fell back, drawing short breaths, my heart banging in my chest. A lion stood amongst the greens, head wreathed by an enormous thicket of hair and crouched in a hunting prowl. It had been killed and stuffed to resemble lifelike instinct and strength. Collecting myself, I climbed back to my feet.

Lions had plagued my nightmares as a boy. I spent much of my childhood looking through my father's books when he wasn't at home. When I was eight, one of the most read articles was of the Tsavo maneaters, a pair of lions that had hunted and killed several railroad workers only three years before in Kenya. I'd always had a morbid fascination with lions;

admiring their appearances and fearing their hunting prowess.

One night, I'd awoken from a dream drenched in sweat, a dream that had been so utterly realistic. The purples in the sky were clear and the feel of the wheaten grass itchy on my skin. I'd been running through the open savannah, blindly zig-zagging to and fro with no knowledge of where I was headed. In my memories, I could still see the lions racing toward me, and the instant futility I'd encountered again and again in dream after dream. I'd curled into a ball as the creature's jaws closed down around my skull.

Awakened by my shouts, my father had come to my room and flung me out of my own bed, yelling at me that my imagination was "dangerous for me". I'd lain there on the floor, stunned and practically in tears. My father had never hit me, but that moment was the most violence he'd ever shown toward me and an act he'd clearly felt justified in committing. My mother consoled me and put me back to bed, though I didn't sleep the remainder of the night.

Staring at this creature reminded me of the similarities between how my father had shouted at me and how Rapp had tried to warn me about the house. They had said the very same thing and instead of taking Rapp's warning as I should have, my knee-jerk reaction had been to get angry instead.

As far as I could tell, the lion before me in the greenhouse was just a taxidermy specimen and nothing more. It hadn't come to life like the Paladin in the dining room. It hadn't reacted to the sound of me falling on the stones, nor had it reacted to seeing me. The king of beasts was in the book, though. There had been an entire page about taxidermy and I remembered seeing "lion" among the list of species. I was unwilling to admit that this might be the first truly harmless thing I had come across since entering the Caulfield estate.

Keeping my eyes on the lion, I crept along the flagstones toward the opposite end of the greenhouse. Not once did the lion move, but his eyes bore holes through me. I tried to see that it was as harmless as the bronze lions in Trafalgar Square, even safer than them. Hell, it was practically a stuffed animal, albeit a large one. I imagined it as a part of Walter Potter's whimsical anthropomorphic dioramas, dressed in a tux, monocle over one of its glass eyes and perhaps playing croquet…

My palms sweated and the scratching of plants against my neck and hands made me twitch. Plants rustled from somewhere deep to my left, but the lion hadn't moved. A sudden paralysis overtook me. I remembered something I'd read in one of my father's books, written by a man who had hunted lions for sport in the darkest heart of Africa. "The male watched and waited while the females did all the work. The females made the ambush."

I ran for the other end of the greenhouse. Vines and fronds whipped my face and arms. The rush of foliage around me was as loud as the current of a roaring river. I awaited the white hot feeling of claws puncturing my skin, that same shock at seeing yellowed teeth and hot sour breath on my face that I'd felt in my dreams as a boy. Each thought tightened my chest until I gasped for breath. Light pierced the jungle and I bumped into the door on the other side of the greenhouse. I scratched at the knob, fingers slipping over the humid metal. I didn't have time! It was going to get me; I was doomed.

The knob turned and I stumbled through. Slipping on the grass outside, I quickly turned and slammed the door closed, the glass juddering under the force. I stared down at my quaking legs, at the grass-stains on my trousers, and at the fog of my breath against the glass door. The swells of vapor expanded with every pant, until I closed my mouth and realized they weren't coming from me.

I glanced up and came face to face with another set of eyes. The glass between us felt like nothing more than air. The lioness had a frustration in her gaze that was palpable, like a heaviness weighting me down. Her instinct and a ravening desire instilled me with a new and all-encompassing fear, where sparks danced in my vision and I momentarily lost control of my own body.

I barely remembered staggering away from the door, vision caught on the silhouettes of not one but three different lithe bodies pacing within the glass world. A guttural roar made the hairs on my arms stand.

There was nothing nearby I could use to barricade the door, and so I was left with no choice but to turn tail and flee the greenhouse and pray the lions didn't decide to smash out of their glass prison.

By the time I stumbled out of the bushes and came face to face with the back of Caulfield manor again, I was frantic. Collapsing in the grass and breathless, I glanced to the setting sun on the horizon. My hope had all but wasted away as I double-checked the time on my watch. I had missed Wolferton's last train and was stuck at Caulfield for the night.

My mouth was dry and cottony. I vaguely remembered being asked on the train if I'd like refreshment and I'd declined, too locked up in my own head to be bothered. I wanted to kick myself for it. My stomach rumbled then and I sighed, realizing just how hungry I was, too. Though I hadn't seen any food or drink inside, I knew there was nothing in the garden besides inedible flowers. I wasn't sure I'd trust anything potentially edible that I might see inside anyway; nothing in there appeared to be what it seemed. But even being hungry and thirsty didn't bother me as much as my desire to reach someone, anyone.

After graduating from university, I'd kept in touch with several friends including my best mate, Aaron. We'd met up every so often at a pub on Portobello Street, share a pitcher of beer (maybe two) and entertain one another with stories of our existences outside of that rigid, didactic template that school provided us. Then the war came. Just like that, our lives were shattered. Aaron and I were the only two who returned from it as some version of our former selves.

I wished I could turn to him now, wished that I had been more specific when I'd talked to him on the phone at the train station. What if he didn't call the police like I'd asked? What if he thought it was a joke? But I knew after a few hours, he'd get tired of waiting. He'd call around, first Frances, then the Post. He'd discover something was amiss. I hadn't told him exactly where I was going but surely once the police were involved, they'd deduce it. They'd call up that drowsy ticket officer from Wolferton and ask him if he'd seen me. It would only be a matter of time then.

Until that happened, I needed to find some kind of shelter for the night and that left only one option: Caulfield.

The thought of being within the house's walls again made me sick to my stomach, but I couldn't remain here in the garden either. I wondered if the lions could still sense me, still smell me from so far away... Now that they knew there was prey for them to hunt, would they break through the plates of glass in the greenhouse? Would they come for me in the darkness when I couldn't see them? If they got out, I'd be at the mercy of their teeth and claws. I couldn't stay here.

A stone veranda bordered the back of the house and two doors beckoned to me from within it. Columns of shadows striped over its seemingly harmless walls. The only way out of here was to go back through the house, back through those perilous doors…

Not wanting to go back in blindly, I opened my father's book and, in the vestiges of dwindling daylight, perused the volume of his hazardous collection. There had to be a map of the house, a key to finding my way out without being eaten or pulverized by these oddities. All it did was serve as a reminder to the other strange things lying inside and the expected horror for what was possibly to come. The sky grew darker and darker, and I squinted as the pages became harder and harder to read.

I turned to a page with a drawing of what appeared to be ordinary spectacles and noticed a stray speck in the center of the illustration. I tried to wipe it away but found it remained where it was. Not dirt; a blue speck of ink. Why there? And it wasn't even black like the entries in the book were. Frowning, I flipped back to the previous page and searched it for a similar mark. This time, it was down in the bottom left-hand corner.

I hunted through the remainder of the book, scrutinizing each page. With each dot that I found, my hope steadily grew and grew. When I had found enough to confirm my suspicion, my mother's kind face emerged in my mind.

She had called it the dot map. Mother would hide chocolates or money around the house on holidays and give me a piece of paper with nothing but dots on it. The number of dots indicated the house level. If one drew a four by four grid of squares on the page, the location of each dot explained the location of the room. Assuming my father had adopted the dot map for his book, it meant that I had some way of telling where I was and where I was going. It also meant that he'd assumed someone would find themselves here in potential danger. Not just anyone though: me. I was the only other person who knew about the dot map. If that was the case, then my father knew he would die and I would come to settle his affairs…

I nearly dropped the book. Had my father known he was going to die? Had he killed himself and destroyed his own research in that fire intentionally? I couldn't accept it. He wouldn't resign himself to a death he knew he could avoid. It didn't make any sense. And that he figured I would come here alone, of my own free will? Well, I suppose I had. But…

Shaking my head, I realized the darkness had fully descended. The lion's roared in the distance and reminded me what would occur if I stayed out here. I had no other choice.

I walked up to the door on the right side of the veranda and forced myself to twist the ornate doorknob with a clammy palm. I pictured my wife telling me that I was safe as she'd done a few days ago at home. Imagining her voice gave me the strength to push in to the hellish house once again.

The room should have been dark. The house had no electricity that I knew of, yet there was light. A bright, alabaster room hurt my eyes upon entering. When they finally adjusted, I saw the room's stark emptiness, the featureless architecture, barren walls, and the vast and purposeless size. There was only the one door that I'd come through and no others.

I turned to leave, deciding I'd take the alternative route through the left door outside on the veranda. The door I'd come through was gone. In its place was another featureless white wall with rectangular outline traced in black paint. I nudged it with my shoulder and pounded my fist against it. It wasn't real. I was trapped.

When I turned back around, another drawn-on door in the opposite corner of the room had appeared. I moved toward it and something crunched under my shoe, the sound thunderous in the empty space. Flecks of white like bits of porcelain covered the floor from where I stood all the way to the opposite wall. I crouched to touch one, and withdrew my hand immediately.

It was a tooth.

They were all teeth: all shapes, all sizes…all seemingly human.

I jumped back, cursing under my breath. A torrent of questions churned in my head. What was this? Why the addition of hundreds of teeth? My father was sick! This proved he was mad!

Now with plenty of light to inspect the book, I desperately thumbed through the pages. I found the image of a tooth displayed prominently and read the passage beneath it out loud:

"The Infected Teeth of the Impalers: Vlad Tepes, often referred to as Vlad the Impaler, was a noted figure in Romanian, Bulgarian, and Transylvanian history and was also Bram Stroker's inspiration for the titular character in his novel, Dracula. During his third reign as Prince of Wallachia in 1476, Vlad and his Moldavian bodyguards were killed by the Turkish army.

"Nearly a century after their death, rumor circulated about the guards' possible infection of a hematological disease. Parish priest, Sorin Albescu, performed a deviant re-burial on them, staking them with metal spikes in the arms, chest, and head. Also a noted denturist, Albescu removed their teeth and kept them in a large jar, using honey as a preservative. Albescu, having renounced his faith before his death, was buried with the jar, believing the teeth had an unhallowed gift of immortality and would reanimate him. His body was exhumed in 1881 and the perfectly preserved teeth were stored in a crypt in the Carpathian Mountains before I acquired them in 1910, taking a detour on my trip to Ankara."

Infected teeth? I put a hand over my mouth. What deadly disease was contained within these bits of ancient bone? I nudged the debris with my foot, to make a clear path.

Shuffling, I made my way to the center of the room, only pushing the teeth out of the way and not stepping on them. There, I stopped. A thick smell had overtaken my senses, like metal and sweet rot, so awful I had to breathe through my mouth.

I closed my eyes. One…two…inhale…exhale… I opened them. You can do this. Just a little—

Something warm dribbled onto my hand. I gazed at the small golden bead and dabbed my finger in it, a string of it pulling away. The smell infected my senses… I brought my hand up to my nose and inhaled it. It was honey.

I glanced up.

A watermark overtook the center of the ceiling. As the seconds passed, it darkened to a rich gold color and expanded over the white paint. Strands dripped down into my hair and I cringed at their warmth against my skull.

I edged my way to the door, trying to avoid the oozing honey as it poured from the ceiling. The stench was almost too much to stand now and I covered my nose with my arm, not knowing what else to do. I reached the painted-on door and pounded on it. It was a solid wall. There weren't any hinges or any cracks in the plaster. I gasped as honey ran down the back of my neck.

Desperately, I opened the book once more and pushed it against the wall to keep it dry as I flipped through the pages. There must have been a clue. There was always a clue with every item. I'd forgotten to check for one!

Honey dribbled down my forehead, into my eye. I smeared it across my face when I tried to wipe it away. Golden beads oozed down the book, gluing the pages together.

A thin layer of honey covered the floor and quickly rose to my ankles within what seemed like a minute. I scratched furiously at the wall. My hand smacked against the imaginary handle and it juddered unexpectedly. Was it real? It couldn't have been. The sticky swipes of honey against the paint had made it almost three dimensional. A hairline crack cut through the plaster where I'd touched the door frame. Drenching my hands in the honey beneath me, I painted the wall with it. The door's features popped and the paint deepened into tangible hinges and an existent outline.

More honey rushed over my hair and down my face. This time, I couldn't wipe it away. My hands and arms were practically drenched. I couldn't see. The honey rose up to my knees and made my movements sluggish. Groping for the door handle, I grasped it, thumbed down the latch, and wrenched hard. My hands slipped and I fell back into the liquid gold.

Memories flooded over me of the war and my post in Passchendaele. Crawling through thick mud, my arms were fatigued, legs quaking, and chest heaving. The sounds of bullets pinged all around. My comrades in arms sunk into the filth around me, their last breaths swallowed by the liquid earth.

You are not going to die here! I sluggishly got to my feet, fought through the honey, and tried for the door again. I hooked my arm around the handle and forced it down, pulling with all my might.

The door scraped against the wall as it gave way. I eased myself through the crack, clutching the book to my chest like a life preserver. The honey spilled in after me. I slipped again, falling on my side into the new room but pulling the door closed after me.

Rubbing at my eyes, trying to clear the honey away, I realized there was nothing in them. I opened them and stared down at myself. No honey. I was completely dry. The floors were pristine and the door behind me was once again a solid wall.

I lay on the floor for a time and caught my breath as I tried to push the memories from the war back into the shadows where they belonged. What had happened in that room couldn't have been my imagination, could it? The honey was so lifelike… I still felt it running down my skin, still taste it where it had touched my lips…

Was I starting to crack? I sat up and put my head in my hands. Could this have all been a dream?

Could I have still been in those trenches up to my eyes in mud and surrounded by slaughter? No, the house was real… Otherwise, all the happiness with my family, all the strife with my father between the war and now was a delusion. My wife wasn't make-believe; my son wasn't fantasy. The honey room had only reminded me of Passchendaele. I wasn't still there. I wasn't imagining all of this. I couldn't have been.

I didn't want to keep going. I'd rather have stayed right there in that hall for the rest of the night, away from any imminent perils. But there were no windows here. I couldn't tell when daybreak came. Even if Aaron was able to call the constabulary and they came here looking for me, they would be at the mercy of the house's other rooms before they could reach me. I didn't want anyone else to suffer from my father's collection, especially if Aaron came with them. God, what if Frances came, too?

On any ordinary evening, Frances and I would be done with dinner by now. She would probably put Emil to bed and read him a story. I imagined her waiting in the hall for me that night; pacing and fretting. Had she forgiven me for not telling her the truth the other day? I didn't know. Last night was the first time we hadn't slept together in the same bed for over a year and the time before was only because she had been dreadfully ill with a cold. What if she wasn't worried about me? What if she thought I'd just gone out to clear my head for the night or something? I'd done so a few times before; driving around in the dark, seeking serenity with myself that was sometimes hard to find. Perhaps she had told Aaron about our fight and now he wasn't coming after all?

Except that I knew my wife; Frances was most assuredly worried. Though she often wore a mask of resolve, I knew Frances thought day and night about our son and our house, her parents, our finances; and lately, a lot about me. She had been under so much strain and I'd been a selfish dolt all week, lost in my own worries about my father and the estate, worries that were justified as it turned out but still...

I got to my feet. I couldn't stay cooped up in this hall. I had to make my own way out. I had to get home to her and Emil. I needed to know she was okay.

Opening the book, I flipped to the page concerning the infected teeth. According to the dot map, it was at the far back of the house. If my calculations about the sizes of the room were correct, it meant there were at least two more rooms that separated me from the front hall where I'd originally entered Caulfield.

I spent several moments flipping through the archives, searching for what could possibly be lying in wait ahead of me. There were so many objects in the book, almost too many to count. It dawned on me that there couldn't possibly be one room for each item. It would stand to reason that if my father had some of these objects shipped elsewhere, there were other places with items in them.

More than one house like this... The thought chilled me. If the dot map covered more than one building, then it was all but useless to try and find my way through Caulfield with it. I had no idea where I was going! I didn't know how to get out of here! I slammed the book shut and threw it as far as I could down the hall. It tumbled to a stop near a wall, the spine up and pages open.

A doorway at the end of the hall beckoned to me. I had to keep going. I had to enter it.

Getting to my feet, I stepped cautiously toward the room. It turned a silvery blue the closer I came, as though it contained some kind of an arctic realm. I gathered the book from the ground and tucked it under my arm as I looked inside.

A polished wooden floor stretched ahead of me, smooth as glass and rich brown in color. Scalloped stellar patterns in the tin ceiling dizzied me the more I looked at them, and inlayed bookshelves filled with black books sat in each corner. Standing in rows on either side of the room were nearly thirty marble sculptures of people, dozens of men and women alike, most of them young and all with their hands up covering their ears. Behind them and in some of the bookshelves rested dusty instruments, everything from a harp that stood at practically my height, to drums, a trumpet, cello...

I remained outside the room, waiting for one of the statues to move. I was convinced that like the lions and the Paladin, they only gave the impression they weren't harmful. Perhaps music made them come to life? Good thing I was rather tone-deaf and a terrible singer to boot. I stayed put for several minutes to study them. They didn't move one inch.

While I shared my father's musical incompetence, my mother had been an accomplished pianist. In one of his rarest compliments, my father had said her skill was impeccable and her compositions lovely anomalies. These strange mélanges could lift him from the darkest of spirits whenever he heard her play. She'd only done so when I was a young lad. As my father spent less time at home, she withdrew from the piano and spent more time in her room. I could still hear her playing Satie and Chopin, her poise as she sat there, the measured way she touched each key and the sound of their pristine harmony.

I realized the sound wasn't only in my memory. From the other end of the room, the faintest plinks of a piano reached out to me. In the shadows, I saw the outline of its grand frame but couldn't see who sat behind it. Stepping past the threshold, I let myself be carried by the familiar tune, a part of me somehow bolstered by it. Those notes reminded me of happier times, of a place in my past that was somewhat peaceful.

I passed the other marble statues, their faces carved in pain, gazes locked toward the ceiling as if begging for release from some higher constitution. I didn't understand why they were covering their ears. The melody was so delightful.

In the center of the room, my vision abruptly clouded over. I put a hand up before me and tried to focus my sight but it waxed in and out. Balance swaying, I careened into a statue, catching myself on its sturdy arms. My legs were beyond my control; my head like a twelve ton stone sitting precariously on my body.

Behind me, the music persisted, chaotic and exquisite. I stumbled back to the center of the room, my hands out at either side as I tried to restore my equilibrium. I plummeted to my knees on the floor, my skull feeling as though it was filling up with cement. The warm trickle of a tear ran down my cheek. As I wiped my eyes with my shirt sleeve, the fabric came away red.

A needle of panic pierced me but quickly faded when I finally saw the piano. Seated at it was a statue of a woman with full cheeks and a demure smile lighting her carved lips. The keys rose and fell on their own away from her hands, neatly folded in her lap. The melody's intensity magnified, the notes clustering together in peculiar yet somehow perfect discord. All I remembered wanting was to become lost in the music; needing to be.

The room dropped away from me as I sank into an abyss of painful pleasure. Everything spun though I remained still, my body light and smoky. Tears coursed down my cheeks. A deeper part of me recognized they were bloodstained and I was oddly fine with it.

I don't know how long I remained locked in that treacly hypnosis. It felt like forever or only a few seconds. A mounting vocal symphony grew from underneath the piano melody, voices that cried out with rhythmic despair. Futility and misery paired together and drained the too wonderful feelings that had blossomed in me because of the piano piece. It was almost as if those voices fought to awaken me…

Managing to open my eyes, the first thing that struck me was my inability to move. The second: I was standing among the other statues.

When I looked down at myself, I gasped. My legs, my stomach, and my right hand had all solidified into marble. I cried out in horror and struggled against the stone prison that was my body. It was no use. I couldn't make my feet budge.

My distress rode the music as if the fear belonged inside of each splendid note. The orchestration desired me to relax and to give up, longed for me to join its gathering of solidified admirers for all eternity. I was tempted, oh so very tempted by the promise of a timeless, delicate embrace.

The voices around me rose and fell. I pictured them as steam, the basses foggy and low to the ground while the sopranos curled into the air higher and higher; clearer and clearer. They called from the statues around me, previous victims of the piano's black widow song. They called for me to resist the music's enticement.

The rock rippled midway up my torso and stopped short of my heart. My chest tightened with it. I didn't have much time. If I stayed here, I'd never be able to leave…permanently trapped in stone. I had to escape…

I fought to focus on a plan, driving my mind to ignore the music. The only way to stop the sounds was to destroy the piano. But how? I was already half frozen in place. I flexed my left hand, my fingers touching my pocket. Something rattled inside. My matches! They were still in there along with my last rolled cigarette. If I could light one and somehow touch it to the piano, I could make the music stop. It was ludicrous plan...unlikely to work…but it was all I had.

Feebly keeping my attention on the task at hand, I willed my hand to reach down into my pocket and grasp the matchbox. Every second felt like agony, my fingers fumbling over it again and again. There! I had it, barely. I tried to concentrate on the statues' voices and ignore the melody. I had to stay in control…just a little longer…

A jangle of piano keys squeezed my lungs closed. I gasped, unable to breathe and in my panic, dropped the matchbook. As the piano's tune intensified, my vision tunneled and my left hand hardened. My heartbeat pounded in my ears and throbbed in my neck, growing slower and slower…

Losing the battle for my mind, I surrendered to the music's glorious abstractions. The hammering in my head loudened, practically shaking the room.

As everything lost its color, the door behind the piano shot open and banged against the inside wall. A figure stomped inside.

Blackness engulfed everything.

Piano keys clanged. Wood squealed and splintered and the music abruptly cut off. The statues' screams rang out even louder. CRUNCH! Some of them stopped abruptly with the smashing of steel on stone.

The cloying spell faded from my thoughts as my vision returned. Air plunged down into my formerly-constricted lungs. I collapsed against the floor and coughed violently as my vision returned.

The room was in a full state of pandemonium. The piano lay demolished. Ivories, strings, and hammers littered the ground around the pummeled carcass. The stone lady sitting at the bench was also broken; the cleaved bottom half still sitting there reservedly.

Above me, the intruder swung a spear around like a crazed destructive force, annihilating every last screaming statue: the Paladin.
I stifled my wheezing and froze in place. What was it doing here? Why had it saved my life?

My confusion promptly lifted as I realized it hadn't, not on purpose. The music had been loud… The Paladin must have heard the piano from the dining room across the manor. He heard it… I knew what happened when the Paladin heard anything. He attacked the source of the sound. Anything within his earshot was at risk, including other items in the collection. Somehow though, he hadn't heard me panting for breath amongst the sounds of his devastation and the statues' screams.

Functioning on primal impulses, I crawled for the doorway, quivering as pieces of rubble crumbled around me and bounced against my body. I closed my eyes and visions of war assaulted me. The repetitive punch of machine gun fire echoed in the thick mists of my memory, the acrid taste of gunpowder in the air; that burnt stench ravaging my nose that I couldn't help but breathe in. Go! Further! Move! The thoughts repeated as I pushed myself onward.

In the corridor outside the music room, I cautiously got to my feet and snuck to the room at the opposite end. The door there was open and undamaged. I slipped inside and closed it behind me as quietly as I could. I leaned there for the longest time, trembling, out of breath and my eyes closed while I battled the memories of what I'd undergone and overcome. Every time I drew a breath, my lungs and throat seared with pain.

You're not at war anymore, Frances's voice whispered against the jagged recollections. *You're safe.* I focused on her face, on her sweet smile and gradually, Passchendaele faded. It wasn't gone, only paled like a stain upon me that I could never wash away. I needed to keep it together, if only for a little longer. I wasn't safe until I was outside of these horrid walls.

One relief shoved to the front of my mind as I took a deep breath and exhaled: The piano was destroyed. No one could be lured by that siren song again, all thanks to that demonic Paladin. Why hadn't he fallen under the piano's spell like I had? I decided I didn't care and wouldn't question any further than that. His immunity to it had saved me from being trapped there forever.

I am alive! I reminded myself. I am almost out of here, almost home to Frances and Emil.

I turned around. Before me was a narrow hall lined with mirrors.

It was from the first page of the book. I glanced down at my hands, preparing to open it up but they were empty. I gasped; I'd left the book behind in the music room.

Cautiously, I put my ear to the door and listened. All had gone silent in the music room. There were no more screams and no more sounds of destruction. I couldn't go back; I couldn't risk the Paladin coming to life again. But somehow, he'd gotten through this room without dying. So could I.

What had the page said? I wracked my brain. Something about fear… Yes, that was it. "Control your fear." I hated the sentence the moment it sprang to my mind. I didn't want to think what would happen if I couldn't harness my fright. I'd barely survived the last room and all I could think of was how I could have died there; how I should have died there. Luck had been my only savior. I doubted I'd have it twice in a row.

You are nearly there, I thought and forced myself to take deep breaths. *You are not afraid.* I walked toward the door at the other end of the room.

You are nearly there and you are not afraid. I pushed the mantra through the torrent of negativity, every dreading cell clashed against my delicate belief that I would be okay. As long as I didn't look into those mirrors with fear in my mind, I would be safe.

I tried to think of the sunlight's warm breath on my skin. I thought about riding through the countryside next to my mother in the car, the softness of her periwinkle blue dress beside me and the shimmers of silver in her hair. We saw vast golden countryside and towns flourishing behind stone fortresses. That one week of delight before she'd died, a chance for my imagination to flourish outside of university, a chance for her to feel free, neither of us smothered in that gloomy estate and by a man who rarely indulged us.

"Open your eyes, Peter."

My mouth fell open at the voice. But when I opened my eyes, there was no one in the room with me.

Spinning, I saw myself in the mirror and froze. Standing behind me in my reflection was my father.

His face was carved with that blend of contempt and disappointment, his skin more craggy than I remembered and his eyes hollower. Was this how he'd looked before he had died? I'd wondered for a time how he'd appear, even imagined what it would be like to see him one last time. He was almost exactly how I'd pictured him.

"Father...?" I could barely move my mouth to speak.

He set his hand on my shoulder. I started in place, shuddering at the pressure of his hand on me, a hand that was nowhere to be seen outside of the reflection. "I am so glad you are alive," he said. "It will be a pleasure to watch him kill you."

I spun around. He wasn't there.

But the Paladin was.

I lurched back and tripped over my own feet as my heart soared into my throat. How? It was impossible! The door to the music room was still closed. He couldn't be here!

The Paladin brandished the mighty spear over his head.

I backed away, but kept an eye on where I moved, willing myself to walk slowly and calmly. All would be fine as long as I didn't make any noise. But, he kept coming, just as slow and just as calm. His bones clicked with each movement, emaciated jaw somehow shaped into a grisly smile.

My composure evaporated. I'm not making any sounds! How does he know where I am? How is he still moving? I glanced over my shoulder for only a moment, noticing I was close to hitting a wall.

The Paladin thrust the spear forward. I leaned back to avoid it, teetering on my heels. The spear shaft swung back and slammed into my chest. The breath I'd fought so hard to regain in the music room was once more knocked out of me. I crashed down onto my back and gnashed my teeth. I heaved for air, my ribs throbbing. This is all wrong! I remembered thinking. Why does he have so much power over me?

As the Paladin towered over me and raised his spear, terror dowsed any lasting hope, a horror I only experienced on the frontlines of war and one that was rooted in nightmares I'd suffered as a child. Visions rushed over me, lying helpless in the grass as a boy, watching the amber eyes of the lions come for me in the violet dark…

A thunderous roar echoed through the mirror room before a gargantuan creature leapt over me. Tackling the Paladin, they crashed to the floor opposite me. I rolled as far away from them as was possible and my breath returned to me at long last.

The lion crouched over the Paladin was even larger than the one I'd seen in the greenhouse. Nose crunched in an ugly snarl, white fangs like blades, and an enormous mane, the beast easily dwarfed the Paladin who struggled underneath. The spear was tucked under the claws of the lion's massive paw. Another roar nearly caved in my ears.

I lay there petrified, having forgotten how to stand. I couldn't focus, drowned in thoughts of my eventual and horrific demise, slaughtered by teeth and claws.

It's not real. The thought punctured through my panic. They're not really here. As the lion ripped into the Paladin's head, I remembered the real Paladin was still in the music room and the door between the two rooms was still closed. This lion wasn't the same one from the greenhouse at the back of the property. It looked over at me, blood-soaked maw dripping and piercing yellow eyes cutting through me. This was all my imagination… None of it was real.

I squeezed my eyes shut and tried to clear my mind by thinking of the only thing that would help me: the book. My priceless and necessary ticket out from this place… I'd left it behind but the mirror could bring it back into existence if I was afraid of it. And afraid of it, I most certainly was. That book had pages upon pages of deadly objects and creatures, its full spectrum largely unexplored. What other monstrous things were depicted within its yellowed pages? I imagined the cracked leather spine and the weight of it in my hands, the sound of the pages flipping open and the cover snapping closed.

When I opened my eyes, the room was empty once more. Rasping, I spun around, searching for any signs of carnage. The floor wasn't bloodstained, the Paladin was no longer broken and flailing on the floor, the gargantuan lion was gone. Only the immaculate mirrors remained. The low light from above gleamed on their golden frames.

My father's book lay at my feet, pristine, as though it hadn't undergone any of the torture that I had. I picked it up in my shaky hands and carefully tucked it under my arm.

Clapping echoed around the space. I stared into the mirror, recognizing the face of my father again, sitting at his desk in his university office behind me. "Well done, Peter," he said, picking up a glass of brandy and downing it.

All that he'd put me through, all of this unnecessary torment, all of the agony, reliving my awful childhood all so I could remember how unavailable, inattentive, and guarded he'd been… He'd made me suffering through my recollections of the war by going through this place and nearly dying one too many times as I did so… My hands balled into fists. "Well done, what?" I spat.

"I never imagined you as a survivor," he said through a cough and poured himself another drink from a glass decanter nearby. "In fact, I never thought you more than an immature dissident."

"And I never considered you'd be mad enough to collect so many horrible things together in one place… We apparently don't know each another at all."

My father clunked the decanter down on the desk and stood. "You were warned not to come here. Inga told you to stay away, but you still came. You brought this on yourself, Peter."

I thought of Rapp on the street that night, her insistence that I not enter the house. How could I not? How could I stay away when she hadn't bothered to explain any of it? My father could have expounded upon his collection in a letter, or could have left it in more capable hands than Rapp's…

I wanted to hit him as hard I could, and the tiny flame of anger deep inside of me surged with that desire. "I came because you kept secrets; like always. This time, it's my responsibility to handle them, because you're not here to."

"Hypocrite," he snarled.

"How?"

"You never cared about my research!" He slammed his glass against the floor.

I shuddered at the earsplitting sound, shards sprinkling at my shoes. "Not before I was obliged to!"

"And your blundering excursion through Caulfield is enough evidence for you to conclude my collection needs dealing with?" He chuckled. "If you'd actually taken the time to read the pages in that book, all of this wouldn't have been such a punishment for you."

I held the book up to the mirror. "How was I to know these words weren't just madness? I believed you had completely lost your mind and I wasn't the only one."

His eyes lost some of their mirth. "As a child, you believed your flights of fancy were real—"

"Until you told me I shouldn't think that way." Now, I turned on my heel to face him, my words like rising like the flame on a torch.

In my amazement, the room around me had changed completely from the hall of mirrors to father's university office. A lone mirror was still behind me, my only distraction from the mirage around me. There my father was, real as ever, watching me with dissecting eyes. I could even smell the sourness of his whisky-tainted breath from where I stood on the other side of the desk.

"When I left for Central America all those years ago," my father said, pushing a hand through his thin grey hair, "never did I dream I would find anything that portended mystic qualities. Never did I imagine there were objects in the world that couldn't be clarified by science, that couldn't be explained without applied principles. I feared I could never truly appreciate the supernatural with my years of rational scholarship and rigid conviction. You were a constant reminder of that blissful ignorance I was missing. How envious I was of you!"

"Envious of me?" I could barely squeak out the words.

"Your ignorance and naiveté; you believed in things that couldn't be seen. I longed for that connection with my effects." He waved his arm at the room. "So much that I bound most of my years to studying them. My work became my life, my purpose to fulfill before my days were over." He looked at me and I saw something akin to humor in his eyes. "When you were older, I thought for a short time, I might even be able to show you. Perhaps this magic might have been a bridge for us to reconnect on. But I gave up on that notion after you went and married that silly girl."

I started from my place but held myself, only just barely. "Frances is my partner, my equal, and my closest friend. After the war, I needed someone I could confide in and confess my spirits to. I wanted the bond that you and Mother once had before you destroyed it."

The wounded look in his eyes was one I'd never seen before and the ire that sprang up after was quick and threatening. I thought he might strike me then. Instead, he turned his back on me and walked to his books to trail his fingers along the rows of spines.

"You're right and you're wrong…" he said. "Mostly right. She was such a delicate creature, your mother. Grace didn't belong with somebody as severe as me; but she made up her mind that she might be able to change the man I was. She couldn't though, not enough. So, she settled for trying to make you into a better one."

I stiffened. "She did that and much more in your absence."

He scoffed but didn't say anything.

"My wife is just as kind and devoted as Mother was. But Frances also has something that Mother never had: the strength to make decisions for her own benefit, regardless of any man's arrogance or self-interest. It's the reason I fell in love with her from the start."

"You're only with her because you worry that someday you'll end up like me. You keep her and the boy around in order to lie to yourself about the kind of man you really are."

The sharp spur of his comment dug in. Such was the anger that coursed through me that I felt I could set everything alight with my eyes if I wanted. "It's true it may be too late to change who I become. But I want to think that someday, if I find myself following your path unconsciously, Frances will have an escape. If I become obsessed to the point of madness, she won't be stuck with me like Mother was with you, like being tied to a rock in a roaring river."

"You don't believe that for a second," my father jeered, walking back to the desk. "All she's done is worried about you ever since you tied the knot."

I nodded. "She worries for me but her endurance is marvelous and I have faith she can hold her own should any horrible self-importance strike me down. She can cut herself free, if need be, and take our son somewhere safe."

He met my gaze. "You and your mother were never forced to stay. I told Grace more than enough times she could leave if she wished, and she should have. But she was set in her ways and she didn't want you to grow up without me."

"I did grow up without you."

"That's what makes it all the worse. You'll never know the wound of shame until you've lost the love and respect of those closest to you."

"Oh, come off it! You outright ignored us and it never bothered you, did it?" I said through clenched teeth.

My father reared his head. "You seem to think I'm nothing more than one of those statues in the music room. Do you think I'm incapable of self-guilt? A man, especially a father, cannot ignore the injustices he's caused his own family. I felt every pain I caused you two. I built them up like a toxin in my body. I never let it show, because what was the point? Nothing useful ever came from spilt tears, nothing except a desire to avoid the mistakes that brought you them. The only way I could keep those ignominies at bay was to avoid you more." While he spoke, he clutched at his chest as though his heart would leap out at any moment.

All of the air left me. For a moment, I thought I'd been turned to stone again. "You are a callous son-of-a-bitch," I whispered.

"That's not a new discovery for you, Peter. If it were, you wouldn't be having this conversation with my phantasm."

I opened my mouth to retort when the words sunk in. It was all an illusion. The walls about me had a dreamlike quality to them, as the books appeared to glow and the world outside the windows was too dark to see properly. The colors around his office seemed too bright and his words were too truthful. My real father would never have revealed anything from beneath his icy exterior. He was dead and this wasn't his ghost I was speaking to; it was an echo of how I remembered him fused with a yearning for closure I'd never experienced. My mind had supplied my father's voice with admissions I'd wanted to hear.

I cleared my throat. "You know there are those who want your collection?"

My father nodded.

"People who are willing to kill to get it?"

"Yes."

"Do you know what they will do with these things if they find them?"

"Yes."

"What?"

My father's gaze lingered on the book in my hands. "Exactly what you think they'll do."

I swallowed the lump in my throat. It was as much a confirmation as I needed, even if it was only a deeper part of me acknowledging it. "Then you know what I have to do."

Again, he nodded.

I turned my back on him, my chest aching although I wished it wouldn't. Nothing had changed between us but I felt different all the same. "Goodbye, Father."

"Peter…" His voice was so brittle, and though the last thing I wanted was to turn back around, to have to look into his eyes once more, I found myself staring at his reflection in the mirror before me one last time.

In a mere blink, my father was abruptly engulfed in fire. His university office burned in the mirror's reflection, doors and windows wreathed by flames, glass melting and books lit like torches. My father stood in the middle of the immolation as though it were a pacifying experience somehow. The temperature suddenly spiked and I whirled around to find the entire hall of mirrors ablaze. I had made the inferno real and now Caulfield house was aflame…

Fumes filled my lungs as I sprinted for the door. Shelves tumbled down behind me and books spilled across the floor like fiery serpents. I wrenched the doorknob to the side and fell headlong into the next room, fully expecting to tumble into another trap, another object's terrible deception. But it was the main hall, the glorious empty main hall that I'd entered hours ago.

Black smoke trailed through the opening while fire licked at the warring parties on the murals overhead. The front door was heavy to open, my lungs wracked by the fumes and my body feverish from the rising heat.

Early morning light spilled across me as I scrambled out. I flung myself down upon the earth outside, coughing and struggling to get further away. The heat intensified as did the gradual roar of the flames as they ate Caulfield's frame, consumed its bricks and bubbled the glass in its windows. I climbed to my feet and stumbled across the lawn.

Once I met the grass at the metal gate, I fell to my knees. Everything I'd experienced collapsed down upon me then; the reality of what I'd witnessed, realizations of what my father had set in motion, the tortures I had barely escaped from. Worst of all was that I could still hear him, his voice resonating in my mind, the things he'd said playing like a static-laced recording. When I closed my eyes, I could still see him burning and hear his screams.

I lost all control and cried out. All of the rage and disgrace and pain that had brewed inside of me upon seeing my father released to the air like the steam from a kettle. I bent my head toward the dirt, fingers clawing at the rich soil, my cries as feral and rending as a wounded animal's. The gunning of engines drew closer over the hills, interspersed with the rapid beeps of a klaxon. Soon it will all be over, a tiny voice inside me said, what I imagined was the last vestigial shred of hope.

It was lying.

*

Pacing and pacing. The room seemed as though it had grown smaller and smaller over the course of the hour. Why was this taking so long?

When I'd awoken, I suspected I would be in police custody, or perhaps a hospital ward. It was a ward, all right, only not the one I'd hoped for. The police had arrived at the engulfed Caulfield manor in their shining black wagon and had apparently tried to put me into the car to take me home. Instead, they found me howling at the sky, unresponsive to their commands. I hadn't gone with them quietly. The local hospital didn't have the resources to deal with someone having an apparent mental breakdown, nor did they want to. The constables brought me to the Ogden Institute instead.

I was pushed into a little room with a man who seemed as old and as jubilant as Father Christmas. Quite looked like him, too, with the thick beard and large gut. Doctor Magorian, his nameplate read. I pleaded my case to him: I had to leave. People were coming for me, people who wanted my father's research and were willing to harm innocents in order to get it.

Magorian sat there with an infuriating calm on his exultant face as he scribbled on a pad of paper at his desk. "Who are these people, Peter?"

I told him. I didn't know who but I knew why.

"Go on," he urged, pen at the ready.

I wasn't cautious. As I paced to and fro, I didn't care how mad I seemed as everything poured out of me. I recalled the churning current of violent and terrible episodes that I didn't want to keep inside any longer. The Paladin, the hall of mirrors, the piano, the lions…

The doctor stopped writing somewhere in the middle of it all and waited patiently until I was done. Then, he asked, "Were you angry with your father?"

I allowed an incredulous chuckle to escape. "Of course I was! It's what I've bally well said, isn't it? He kept all of these things at Caulfield and never told me. But that's what they wanted. I'm the only one who knows about his collection now."

"Did you feel the same rage toward Ms. Rapp?"

"W-what is the matter with you?" I stammered. "Aren't you listening to me? She was a part of it. They bloody killed her because she was!"

Magorian folded his hands together in his lap. "Who are 'they' again, Peter?"

I took a step toward him. "Good God, man, I told you; I don't know!"

"Did your feelings toward your father compel you to burn down Caulfield House?"

I grabbed the back of the chair in front of his desk, my knuckles turning white. "I don't have time for this. I have to get home. My family is in danger!"

He coughed. "You'll return to your wife and son in due time, Peter. We only want to make sure you're healthy in mind as well as in body."

"Healthy?" The word came out as barely a whisper. "I've just barely survived being eaten, and skewered on a spear, and…and being burned alive! I'd say being "healthy" is the absolute least of my worries at the moment."

His smile only widened. "I would like you to follow Nurse Hull to a room where you can gather yourself. We'll come to collect you when you can leave."

I trailed a woman with all the grace and fluidity of a primordial beast to the tiny cell-like room. She left me there for over an hour; perhaps two. All the while, my thoughts raced and my pacing grew more frantic. I tried the door only to find it locked from the outside. The clock was ticking. Frances and Emil weren't safe on their own. I briefly wondered why my wife hadn't come for me. Surely, she would have cleared this entire situation up. She knew the kind of man my father was; she knew who I was.

Digging my fingers through my hair, I turned as the lock clicked back. Hull opened the door, her curved nose and beady, light-colored eyes fixed on me like a raptor having spotted its prey. "Come with me, Mr. Dawson."

My spirits soared as I followed her in the hall. At last, Frances had come. She was safe!

We walked for a time, each hallway seeming whiter and longer than the last. I was pretty sure we'd passed the main foyer but didn't speak up. I didn't know how these kinds of facilities released patients, not that I was ready to admit I was one. Perhaps there was another door where I would meet my wife.

Hull entered an open room and I joined her inside. My legs faltered. There was no exit, no promise of departure, and no Frances. A gurney sat near the wall dressed with a rubber sheet. Thick blankets were folded on a table next to a metal wash bin with linens in it. Beyond them was a porcelain tub, brightened by a large window where daylight burst in like a scream.

I collected my voice. "What is this?"

"It's called hydrotherapy, Mr. Dawson. It will leave you feeling relaxed and help to calm that anxiety of yours."

"No." I stepped away. "The doctor said I could leave. Frances will wonder where I am."

"Your wife has been informed about your condition," Hull explained, reaching out to me.

"My condition?"

"We believe it is schizophrenia. But not to worry, we'll take good care of you here." She curled her fingers around my arm. "Now, what you need is a cold pack to take your mind off all this nonsense about living statues and gyrating libraries."

I pried her fingers off me. "What happened to me was real. What do I have to say so that you'll believe me?"

Doctor Magorian stepped into the room from another door. "You're confused, Mr. Dawson. Anyone would be after what you experienced."

The way he talked, they talked, was too calm and too collected.

"No…"

I turned to leave, but bumped straight into another man, a tall orderly with ruddy cheeks and gawky arms and legs. He blocked the doorway.

I backed into the room and glanced at each of them. "There's been a mistake. Please."

"Your episode at Caulfield leads us to believe you've developed a paranoid precocious madness. Your father's questionable mental health was common knowledge and we think it could be genetic. Treatment is necessary to keep you from following a similarly destructive path," the doctor said.

I flinched. "I'm nothing like my father."

Again, Hull reached to take my arm.

I snatched my hand away. "Get off me!"

The orderly advanced on me and I backed away from him into the room, further and further from my only exit.

Magorian put up his hands. "Easy, Peter. We don't want to hurt you."

I bumped into something; the bathtub. I'd gone further than I'd wanted to.

Hull's petite eyes were cold and dead, their effect gorgonizing me in place. "But we will if we must."

The realization collapsed down on me. Witnesses had seen a tall gangling man push Rapp into traffic. I stared at the orderly; I gazed at his long limbs like the crooked twists of four tree branches, at how he leered over me like some behemoth waiting to devour its trapped victim. "You killed her, didn't you?" I glanced at Magorian and Hull. "You're with them."

The orderly seized my arms with iron fingers and easily flipped me off my feet into the tub. I gasped as glacial liquid swallowed me. Water and lumps of ice gushed into my open mouth. Instinct took over as I kicked and clawed at his savage grip on me. No matter how I thrashed, I couldn't loosen his hold; his strength was inhuman. My lungs gave out and more water rushed in.

The orderly heaved me out of the ice bath, and I half-crawled into his arms to let him, sputtering and choking. Grappling me from behind, he hooked his spider-like arms under mine and pulled them back to keep me from escaping. Even as shock assailed me, I desperately fought against his hold. Hull appeared at my side and slipped a needle into my arm.

A strange warmth overtook me as I was heaved on a gurney. It wasn't enough to calm my violent shivering. Even the orderly's hold couldn't still me as I struggled to break free. He and Hull peeled my wet clothes away piece by piece and discarded them somewhere outside my periphery. Terror sliced its way across my mind like a hunted man chopping through a jungle with a machete. I shouted at the top of my lungs, calling to anyone that might be near.

A horrible dampness tightened across my chest and limbs as Hull rolled my body into a wet sheet and tucked in the sides around me. Together, she and the orderly brought another layer around me, and secured it to the bed. I writhed against the confinement but couldn't move. The sheets were so constricting, I couldn't even ball my fists.

Hull draped a wool blanket up around my neck, puckering it in on both sides of the mattress. Another was pulled up around my body. And another. The cocoon completed, she wrung out a small towel over the wash bin and draped it over my forehead. It, too, was freezing, but I couldn't shrink away. She stepped back to admire her work.

"Let me go!" I yelled. Claustrophobia swept in like a first frost. Recalling the music room at Caulfield and my near-death experience there, I bucked as hard as I could. It was no use; I was mummified. With my entire body confined against the mattress, I couldn't budge.

"Monitor him for three hours, make sure he's calm. Then, do the treatment again," Magorian ordered before he moved into my eyesight. "Rest, Peter. Soon, you'll feel much better," he said with an insidious grin.

I could barely form words on my lips. Exhaustion and the medicine tugged my mind down toward the sludgy mire of slumber. "You bastard."

He disappeared from my vision and I heard the door close behind him as he left.

So cold. Get warm. Stay awake.

My mind had shut down to the point where only those visceral impulses echoed. A nauseating calm invaded them as minutes passed and the drugs coursed through my veins. Oblivion lurked beyond the edges of my sight, waiting to close in.

Stay awake.

The deadly cold was soon supplanted by an uncomfortable and escalating heat. Wrapped in so many clammy blankets was like being cramped in a tiny box filled with tepid water. I practically suffocated from the warmth. Sweat beaded on my neck, beneath my arms and soon, all over. Ember-like flares of light sparked up and danced across my vision while dizziness rocked over me, the room tipping back and forth, back and forth...

I slipped into sleep against my will, into a blackness I wasn't sure if I'd ever wake from.

*

"Peter?"

Frances had said my name five times in the last minute and still, I couldn't make eye contact with her. For the longest time, I wasn't sure if I was hallucinating again or if she was really there. Her persistence convinced me she was genuine.

She shouldn't have had to come in a place like Ogden. It wasn't dignified for her. It smelled of piss and sorrow, wreaked of madness. The police had assumed I was mad, too. They couldn't believe in the Collection. To them, I had burned down my father's estate in hysteria, driven by feelings of ill-contempt for him, feelings of rage and vengeance.

An old man began to urinate against the wall close by. The orderlies wouldn't go near him yet. Instead, they hung back like the great watch dogs they were so they could drag him back into a dingy cell as soon as he was done.

"Peter…please." Frances's voice was more desperate. I hated her being subjected to this place. But I needed her. She was my only hope of escaping Ogden alive.

This faceless organization that desired my father's secrets had won. They'd muzzled me and pronounced me insane to keep me from telling the world about them. Hull and Magorian and especially, their Cerberus orderly; they were not who they said they were. They had killed Rapp and covered up her death, drove my father to destroy his research and himself… I feared to think what else they were capable of and how large their organization truly was.

I'd endured three cold packs my first day at the institute. Left on the bed for hours at a time, the sheets tightened as they dried which pinched and crushed my fevered body. When I started to awaken, Hull and the arachnid orderly dumped me back into the ice cold water and left me shivering on the gurney to repeat the torturous process again. I'd learned the orderly's name at this time: Borg, a name that felt acrid yet clumsy on the tongue, a name appropriate for his awkward frame and monstrous countenance.

After the treatments were over, Borg discarded me in the same room where I was left when I'd arrived. I lay in a heap at the foot of the bed, too delirious and ill to move. In the night, I awoke, having gained some of my energy back. I called for help as loud as I could. Perhaps there were genuine doctors and nurses here that could help me if only they knew what was going on. Someone had to hear me! Someone had to take pity…

My shouts awoke several others and pandemonium ensued as the entire hall joined in with me. My anticipation flew, and for a few brief minutes, I was convinced that the riot I'd started would bring someone outside of Magorian's schemes to my room.

Unfortunately, Hull and Borg reached my room before anyone else could. They couldn't risk me telling anyone what they'd done; they needed me kept silent. Borg grappled me down onto the floor and Hull injected me with a cocktail of clear fluids that instantly made me groggy. I had no sense of time on these medicines and slept away entire days, kept under on a constant sequence of pills. I'd wake here and there, barely registering whether it was morning or night, always with confusion about what had happened and where I was.

In my few coherent moments, Hull and Magorian were always nearby, either counting out another dose or writing down observations. I almost never ate and what I did never managed to stay down. I barely used my bed pan for more than vomiting. As the days passed, hunger weakened me and the onset of a terrible fever left me with chills, hallucinations, and a worsening cough.

Frances assumed the Ogden Institute was helping me. She had no idea who Magorian and his associates really were, didn't recognize that my downward spiral wasn't mental; it was completely pharmaceutical. Magorian's goal was to drive me into lunacy and eventually, to death with his drugs. If I kept receiving them, I knew someday I'd cease to wake up.

"I'm here for you, Peter," Frances's voice trembled. "But you have got to come out of this stupor. Tell me what happened to you! Tell me what's made you so ill. I need to know you'll come back to me; to your son. You have to give me something to work with."

All I could do was shiver. Trapped inside of my own fevered body, my mind fought for control. It was as though I was underwater, looking up at myself floundering on the surface.

That morning, in a rare clear moment of judgement, I had refused my treatment. Borg locked me in four point restraints on my bed while Hull injected me anyway. Hours later when Frances came to visit me, they'd wheeled me in to a common room like an invalid. I was only free from my manacles because I could barely move, let alone keep my eyes on my wife. Focusing on her words was especially difficult.

Frances cleared her throat and sniffed. She didn't like to cry. In that way, her and my father were very alike. Even now, I could see she was unable to hold it back. "Someone came to the house the other day," she said. "He asked about your father, some kind of research he was doing and a book… I told him to leave and he wouldn't go! He was horrible, Peter. A frightful man with a terrible smile… I thought he was going to force himself inside. Aaron showed up in the nick of time and only by chance. The man seemed very upset when he left." She shivered. "I'm frightened, Peter. I think he'll be back."

The burst of dread entered my bloodstream at her words. Had Magorian been to my home? Why would he have looked for the book there? I'd had it with me when the police took me into custody. No, I didn't have it when I came to the institute. I must have left it at the house. Or perhaps the police still had it. Whatever the case, Magorian was closing in. If he thought Frances possessed it, she and Emil were in danger.

She dabbed at her eyes as tears fell. "We need you. Please come back to us."

My chest ached. I longed to touch her hair, to tell her I was there to protect her. I scratched at the glassy shell that held my mind in that hellish torpor. I needed release! I needed her to know she wasn't alone!

Frances sighed. "I'm afraid I can't stay any longer, Peter. Aaron and Molly are waiting for me outside. They gave me a lift. They wanted to come in but…" She let the sentence hang and I recognized the lie in it. They hadn't wanted to come in. They didn't want to see me like this.

Frances looked to the ceiling. "Please, God, help him," she muttered under her breath before looking at me in the eyes again. That gaze sent ripples of misery through me. "Goodbye, my love."

Instinct bolted through me. The shell cracked. I tried to lift my arm to grab her hand before she could go, but it didn't move.

She stood and began to walk away.

"Nnnno!"

She spun around. "Peter?"

My voice! Had that been my voice? It sounded nothing like I remembered; weak and hoarse, but it was real! Before I could speak again, my chest seized and I crumpled in my chair as fits of coughs overwhelmed me.

She rushed back to me. "Goodness, darling, are you alright?"

Again, old boy. You can do this. "D-d-don't…" My whole face was numb; my jaw juddered with effort. Come on, come on! "…leave m-me here."

"Thank the lord, you've said something!" Frances sat back down and grabbed my hands. Hers were so warm. "Oh, your fingers are like ice!"

"F-Frances." It was coming easier now, slowly but surely. Her smile reminded me of a delicate slice of the moon. I imagined the soft lunar glow in her hair, of her smooth skin in my embrace, tucked close to me as we slept. I used it as a ladder to pull myself out of the suffocating deadness the medicine had put me in. "G-get me out of here."

"You're sick, Peter. The doctors said you've been unresponsive for nearly a week. They're only trying to help—"

"They d-did this to m-me."

A haunted look crossed her face. "What?"

"The d-drugs are k-killing me."

She blinked slowly. "Your nurse? Hull or something? She said you were confused…"

I shook my head wildly.

"Peter…"

"You kn-know me," I said.

"You need to rest. You can hardly talk."

I closed my eyes, my frustration unhinging. "P-please listen to me!"

"Alright." Frances stilled. That collectedness that I admired so much about her shone in her face as she leaned in. "I'm listening."

Tears welled up in my eyes and soon, I tasted salt on my tongue. "I'm t-telling you I am not cr-crazy. Th-that man who c-came to the house… Th-that was my doctor."

Her mouth dropped open a little. "How could you know that, Peter?"

"Th-there's a ph-photo over th-there." I nudged my head toward a picture on the wall.

Frances cautiously stood and moved toward the group portrait hanging across the room. She got up on her tip-toes and inspected it closely. After a moment, she put a hand to her mouth and glanced back at me.

I nodded.

She rejoined me at the table. "It's him!"

"He's d-dangerous. He's had th-them keep me asleep f-for days."

"Days?" Her eyes widened. "Why?"

"I d-don't…I don't…" I lost control. Sobs racked me. It was so hard to think, so hard to organize my thoughts. All I wanted was for her to understand me, for her to take me out of here. But I needed to be able to talk to explain to her why!

"Darling, calm down." She came around the table and crouched in front of me, combing her fingers through my hair. As soon as she started, she snatched her hand away. "You're damp." She pressed the back of her hand to my forehead. "Oh, darling, you're burning up!"

"I'm so cold…" I lost my voice in another spasm of coughs.

"Peter, how long have you been like this? Haven't they done anything for you?"

Hull's crone-like figure approached us out of the corner of my eye. I saw the pills in her knobby hands and my hope evaporated. "It's time for your medication, Mr. Dawson," she droned.

I shrunk deeper into my chair.

Frances stood abruptly and stepped between me and the nurse. "You will not put any more of that poison into my husband, let alone touch him again." Her words were direct, her tone deadly. I'd only heard her speak that way a couple times before, but never with that level of fury.

Innocence, no doubt feigned, filled Hull's eyes as she held her ground. "I'm afraid it's a part of his treatment, Mrs. Dawson. Don't you want him to get better?"

"He isn't getting better; only worse. He has a fever and he can barely speak!"

Hull nodded. "He suffered a trauma in that house, deary. He's very, very ill."

"No," I begged. "Th-that's what they want you to think."

Frances didn't look at me, her fiery gaze narrowed on Hull. "I'll be removing my husband from your care immediately. I shall need to speak with your administrator as soon as possible."

Hull's mouth puckered a little. "It's not as simple as that. There are procedures that must be—"

"I suggest you make it simple," Frances demanded. "My uncle serves on the Board of Control for Lunacy and Mental Deficiency. I can be through to him in one phone call and have the Lord Chancellor here within a day. Is that what you want?"

Hull staggered back; she actually staggered back! "He'll need a doctor to sign his release papers and unfortunately, no one here believes he is of sound mind. He isn't fit to return to society."

"Not to worry, I know a doctor." Frances turned to another younger nurse at the desk across the room. "You there. If you could, please put in a call Doctor Wilbur Thurman at Hertford College at Oxford. It's an emergency and I need him at Ogden Institute straight away."

The nurse dutifully nodded and picked up the receiver on the phone nearby.

"This is highly irregular, ma'am," Hull said, scoffing. Her eyes flicked back and forth and I could see her control on the situation slipping through her fingers. Other visitors in the room had begun to stare now. A few of the orderlies were now watching Hull in a questioning way. Innocent bystanders were the only thing keeping Frances safe right now, I knew.

"Nothing as irregular as forcing a man who claims he isn't crazy into a coma for a week and then not attending to his well-being." Frances snapped. "I have nothing more to discuss with you. Leave us."

Hull walked stiffly out of the room, no doubt to find someone else to abuse.

My champion, my Frances. I could scarcely believe she'd pulled it off! She knelt by my wheelchair and clutched my hand in hers. "I won't let you out of my sight," she promised.

Exhausted from the effort to break through the drugs, I leaned back in my seat and sighed with relief. "I'm l-lucky you're so fierce."

A sad smile overtook her features. "When it comes to keeping you out of trouble, I can be as ferocious as need be."

"This uncle of yours? I d-don't rem-remember him."

"You wouldn't." She gazed up at me unblinkingly.

I closed my eyes. "You are brilliant."

She leaned in and pressed her forehead to mine.

I could have stayed forever that way. If there was ever a moment in time that I could pause, it would be there; the affection, pride, and gratitude I had for my wife then was beyond words.

"Dr. Wilbur Thurman is on the line for you, madam," the young nurse called.

"Go," I whispered to her.

"We'll have you out of here in no time," she said, and walked over to retrieve the telephone.

I glanced out the window toward the front walk of the institute, lashed with rain. I was already considering where we would need to go in order to escape my father's enemies. Clearly, Magorian and the rest of his ilk wouldn't be satisfied until they had a copy of "The Collection" in their hands. That meant either finding the book I'd left at the house, or keeping me in their clutches, the only living person who had seen it.

There was only one place far enough away from their grasp: the American house; Hiraeth. The other estate my father had left to me in his will. Hiraeth was the place for us to start over, his gift to me knowing there would be people coming for his secrets. It would have been over if the Collection had all been at Caulfield. I was the only witness to the terrible things he'd kept there, and I had destroyed them all. But, the book's objects weren't just at Caulfield. There were other secret places that he'd kept these horrors and I still had no idea where.

It didn't occur to me then that Hiraeth could be a lingering trap, that my father could have kept items for the collection there. True to its name, Hiraeth was wistfulness for a home I hadn't been able to return to, a place of lovely and serene nostalgia that I yearned for in a way I'd never experienced. To me, America was our only hope. The house in Seraphim City was to be our rebirth.

I never suspected it would end up being our ultimate descent into obsession and madness.

Acknowledgements

I'd like to thank first and foremost my editor, Tanya Gold, for being so supportive and ecstatic about this project, for your expertise and time in helping me to see new avenues that this story could take. This project wouldn't have been completed without support from a wonderful writing group who spent time and energy giving me feedback, suggestions, and helpful critiques. Thank you, Emily Randolph, Kalani Palm, and A.J. Dodge for all of your input. And last, but certainly not least, thank you to my close friends, my family, and my wonderful boyfriend for keeping me going. Five years felt like a long stretch and it feels so, so good to see this story come to life in published form.

Interview with the Author

How did "The Collection" start? In 2013, I'd written a five page teaser about a character in a lawyer's office receiving an inheritance from his dead father. It started off as more of a comedic piece and got a lot of good response at readings. I didn't have much of a plan for it at that point.

When did the first idea about turning it into a horror story happen? I had a pretty strange dream after one of my readings where I was wandering around a large estate. It seemed a little run down, as if no one lived there anymore. I remember distinctly that I entered an outbuilding of some kind and in the glowing afternoon light, saw a whole collection of taxidermy animals, notably big cats. After I left, I had looked over my shoulder and some of them had begun to move. The idea of living taxidermy stayed with me and I really wanted to integrate that scene into this story.

What were some of your inspirations while writing? I had fallen in love with Downton Abbey some time ago and really felt the post WWI/Edwardian era fit this story. In turn, I had also picked up this awesome mini-series called "The Lost Room" from a Movie Gallery that was closing down. The series is about a bunch of objects with extraordinary abilities created by an unknown event and revolves around one ordinary man's exposure to them. I really liked the concept of an unknown number of these objects existing and that their history was a bit nebulous and I thought, "Wouldn't it be cool if someone collected these things into a kind of hellish museum?"

Why write a novella and not a full novel? This project always felt like it would be a short one to me from the beginning. I didn't envision it being a really in depth piece until I wrote my third book in the Monstrum Chronicles series. For those that don't know (everyone, haha), there is a tie-in with my Monstrum Chronicles series. The house featured in Book 3, is owned by the Dawson family and items from the Collection appear in that book.

I started thinking that it would be fun to write a sequel to The Collection and a prequel to Memento Mori, wherein the Dawson family moves to the United States and into this house there. It would be conceptually more like Downton Abbey meets American Horror Story and that really invigorated me. Presently, I have about a third of that novel written and the whole thing plotted out.

How long did it take you to write "The Collection"? Five years. For a book that's less than 100 pages. Call me crazy, but this is probably one of the hardest things I've written yet.

What music did you listen to while writing? With this book, I stayed purely instrumental. A lot of influences came from the work of James Newton Howard, the soundtrack from a lovely little indie game by the name of Tormentum: Dark Sorrows, Dario Marianelli, Max Richter, and several others. If you are interested in viewing the full playlist, you can check it out at katherinesilvaauthor.com.

Last question: what object in the Collection scared you the most? The piano, hands down. Writing that part was intense.

ABOUT THE AUTHOR

Katherine Silva is a Maine author of dark fiction, a connoisseur of coffee, and victim of cat shenanigans. She is a two-time Maine Literary Award finalist for speculative fiction and a member of the Horror Writers of Maine, The Horror Writers Association, and New England Horror Writers Association. Katherine is also a founder of Strange Wilds Press, Dark Taiga Creative Writing Consultations, and The Kat at Night Blog. Her latest book, *The Wild Dark*, is now available wherever books are sold.

Learn more about her at katherinesilvaauthor.com

Made in the USA
Middletown, DE
15 March 2022

62620238R00076